The Peasmarsh Players

CR Gilfillan

The Peasmarsh Players

Book 3 of the Rags Whistledown North Norfolk Series

Cowslip

Published by Cowslip Press

Cowslip

9 Casson Street
Ulverston
LA12 7JQ

First Published in 2020

Cataloguing in Publication Data for this book
is available from the British Library.

ISBN 978 1 9996097 6 4

Also available as an ebook ISBN 978 1 9996097 5 7

Designed and formatted by Russell Holden at Pixel Tweaks
www.pixeltweakspublications.com

To Heather de Lyon and Zosia Wand
- *my faithful readers*

Cast of Characters

The Peasmarsh Players

Hengist Bright: Chairman and Director of *Jeeves Pulls it Off*
Mindy Bright, his wife: Administrator and Vice-Chair
Iain Bright, their son: a member of The Peasmarsh Players
Cedric Williams: a member of The Peasmarsh Players
Janette Tinker: a member of The Peasmarsh Players
Betzy Stretch: a member of The Peasmarsh Players
Dave Bennett: a member of The Peasmarsh Players
Alfie Adams: a member of The Peasmarsh Players
Toots Riley: wardrobe mistress for The Peasmarsh Players
Jem Townley: carpenter, boyfriend of Janette Tinker, set builder for The Peasmarsh Players

Other Residents of Wells-next-the-Sea and Fakenham

Rags Whistledown: journalist and private investigator
Graham Whistledown: Rags' father, retired, living in Fakenham
Gwendolyn Vickers: Rags' mother, married to Nigel Vickers
Tarquin Vickers: Rags' step-brother, the son of Gwendolyn and Nigel
Susie Smith: Graham's partner
Tracey Jones: Graham's neighbour

Residents of Peasmarsh or connected with St Botolph's

The Reverend Hugh Blackthorn: vicar of St Botolph's and two other small parishes
Evangeline Nielsen: administrator of St Botolph's and two other small parishes
Zillah Lloyd: a young woman living temporarily in the flat attached to St Botolph's
Bert: living in sheltered housing beside the church
Andrea: his daughter
Edward: a friend of Bert's, keen to be of assistance to Rags
Characters from Norwich
Julian (previously Julie) Lloyd: Zillah's mother, living in The Sistren community in Norwich
Laurie: a friend of Zillah's
Marianne: a worker at A Place to Call Home, the Norwich shelter where Zillah has volunteered

1

In which Rags gets her arm twisted

Dad rang while I was strolling down the quay at Wells-next-the-Sea

'Are you coming to the auditions, then?'

I groaned. 'I don't know, Dad. Amateur dramatics are not really my thing.'

'Come on! We're all meeting up in the pub first. The Peasmarsh Players are a good crowd, and they're desperate for young blood.'

'I don't know if I qualify as young,' I said, flattered nonetheless to be categorised as youthful at the age of 43.

'You're young compared to most of them.'

'But I can't act! Don't you remember how terrible I was as an angel in the nativity play?'

'You were very good, if I remember rightly. It wasn't your fault you got knocked over by the donkey. But they're not really looking for actors – they've got plenty of them. They need people to help out with other things. Susie gets involved with publicity and selling tickets. And I'm going to turn my hand to a bit of carpentry – help out with the set.'

'Oh, all right,' I said, mainly to please him, and because he was so happy to be romantically involved with Susie, his new partner.

'Fantastic. We'll pick you up at half six.'

We said our goodbyes. As I hung up I wondered how I'd let myself be talked into that. I had other things to do – lots of them, because I'd moved into a flat in Wells-next-the-Sea three days before, and had some serious home-making to get on with.

If I peeped out of the skylight in my bedroom I could see the curve of the channel running from the harbour to the open sea. The murmur of waves breaking beyond the sage of the salt marsh rolled up Staithe Street, carrying on its back the scent of salt and the cries of gulls. It was mid-September, three months after I'd landed on Dad's doorstep with my suitcase, guitar, and a ton of debts, having been evicted from my London flat over the small matter of nearly five grand of rent arrears I'd accrued after my money-grabbing landlord doubled the rent.

Since then I'd solved a murder case and set myself up in business as a private investigator. I was recently back from a couple of weeks' work on the Cote d'Azur and had returned with enough money to pay off most of my debts and buy a pre-loved Peugeot to carry me round the lanes of North Norfolk.

Life was pretty damn good.

With a sigh I let myself fall back on the big, comfortable bed I'd picked up at Fakenham auction. Through a stroke of good luck (several, actually) I'd been offered a six-month lease on this property – a flat in need of major updating owned by a friend of Dad's who didn't yet have the funds to repair the boiler and replace the windows. Yes, I'd need to build a fire and wear several jumpers when the chilly fist of winter closed in, but the flat was mine for a modest rent in return for keeping it warm and dry. I'd loved staying with Dad, but he had a new relationship and needed some privacy.

As for me? I'd spent a blissful couple of months with Alaric, an eco-dude living on Dad's street, but he was now working in India, and we'd decided to put our love affair on hold.

So I was single and fancy-free.

2

In which we meet members of The Peasmarsh Players

Hengist Bright

At 3.45 pm, in the office that occupied the fourth bedroom of his modern, austere house, Hengist Bright settled down at his Scandinavian pine desk. In front of him was an Apple MacBook, but he didn't open it. Instead he slid it away and reached for a sheet of thick, cream paper. He loved the feel of the paper – the weight of it and its subtle water mark. He noticed things like that. He knew about *quality*. The house was quiet, with just the distant thrum of the sea drifting in the open window. Mindy, his wife, was on her way back from Brussels and would be home within the next hour, and though he'd be sorry to relinquish his solitude, he was grateful she'd be there to organise his production of *Jeeves Pulls it Off*.

That would leave him free to focus exclusively on his creative vision. He was determined to capture the essence of P G Wodehouse – the light-hearted fun of Jeeves and Wooster, and the gentle satirical digs at upper-class society.

Yes, it was frothy, but he knew that one of the judges of the regional competition for amateur productions was a P G Wodehouse fanatic. And Hengist was determined to win the competition this year; he didn't like to come second. Only winning was good enough for him.

He ran a clean fingertip down the list written in purple ink, hovering over each name, feeling a frisson of pleasure when he lightly touched certain ones. His mouth curved into a smile. He took a sip of mineral water flavoured with slices of cucumber and lime. Casting required vision. It required ruthlessness. Some people would be disappointed, but that was too bad. Handling their reactions came with the role of artistic director. You needed someone bold, visionary, to run this sort of outfit. Someone firm. Someone like him.

Particularly now, when so much was at stake.

It was a shame he had this *other* thing to deal with. He didn't like to be distracted from his vision, his purpose.

Nevertheless, he'd have to do *something*.

* *

Alfie Adams

In his cavernous en-suite bedroom at Wrigton Hall, five miles from Wells, Alfie Adams perused himself in the speckled mirror, and straightened the parting in his hair. There: that was better. He lifted his chin, raised an eyebrow. Bloody perfect! If he didn't get the part of Bertie Wooster in *Jeeves Pulls it Off* he'd eat his hat. He just had to convince Hengist – persuade him that the little mishap that had occurred during the run of *All My Sons* wouldn't happen again. To prove that he was worthy of the role, he'd been rehearsing Bertie's accent and mannerisms, so he'd be able to deliver a performance rather than a reading at the audition. That would impress Hengist, wouldn't it?

It was a shame Hengist was such a miserable git. He was a complete and utter killjoy. No drinking, no smoking of dope or tobacco during rehearsals and before shows. It was amazing he let them drink coffee. Oh, it was easy enough for Hengist: he seldom sipped anything other than water and subsisted on a vegan diet. He didn't understand that giving up the little pleasures of life could be a struggle for lesser mortals.

Oh shit! A frown line had appeared between his eyebrows. Alfie smoothed his face into an amiable smile until he was satisfied with his reflection once more.

Right. He adopted a languid pose and started to run through the first scene with Jeeves, the butler infinitely more clever than Bertie Wooster. After a moment he clenched his fists and let out a cry of frustration because he was still stumbling over the lines. He glanced over at his sock drawer, feeling the pull of what was in there. After a brief tussle with himself he rushed over and pulled the drawer open. Hidden at the back was a small bag of amphetamine sulphate (speed), his preferred pick-me-up – cheaper and swifter acting than cocaine. Looking over his shoulder (though Ma was banging around in the kitchen and wasn't going to barge in) he laid out two lines and snorted them through a silver straw one of his exes had given him as a Valentine's Day gift. An icy tingle raced through his nervous system, ending with a mini explosion somewhere in his skull. He straightened up, went to the wash basin and carefully washed his face so no trace of powder remained. Then, as his brain revved up, he released a breath of relief. That was better. That would help him stay on top of his performance.

He checked his phone: six o'clock. Time to get changed. He pulled off his comfortable old jeans and tugged on a pair of flannel Oxford bags and a spotless shirt. Laced up a pair of gleaming patent leather shoes. Returning to the mirror he checked his appearance again. Appearances were *everything* – he'd learned that early on, at school, where he discovered that though he wasn't the brightest spark, he got better marks if he showed his best profile, wore nice clothes and smiled at the teachers.

Humming *Cheek to Cheek* he adjusted his shirt collar. It was a shame there was an ugly crease running across it, but the woman who did the laundry and cleaning for Blue Sky Cottages, the holiday lets on the estate, drove the steam iron as if it were a Sherman tank, adding creases where no creases should be, and powering into buttons so they hung loose from their threads. These manoeuvres were carried out with moronic Radio 2 blaring beside her. When he'd tried to speak to her about the offending creases in his shirts she'd fixed him with her mono-brow frown and said that if he could do better he was welcome to try.

He fiddled with the shirt collar until it fell casually open at the neck in a way that disguised the hideous crease.

A tap on the door disturbed his composure. 'Can I come in?' The door opened before he could reply and Ma barged in with a cup of coffee and two Florentines on a black-lacquer tray. 'Oh! You look so dashing.'

'You're too kind,' he said, practising his upper-class drawl (not so different from his own accent, though he affected a Thames estuary twang when he went into London to meet up with old school pals who were slumming it in the East End.) As he gazed in the mirror, twitching a lock of hair into place, he could feel her adoring gaze on his back, provoking the usual prickle of irritation so sharp it was painful. Ma was devoted – always had been. His poor old sis, Beatrice, ten years his senior, had been ignored ever since he was born in an exclusive private hospital on the outskirts of Norwich. Since then Ma's attention had been focused on her son to the exclusion of all else. Beatrice had been packed off to some third-rate boarding school, but Ma had had a screaming fit when Pa suggested Alfie be incarcerated in the same sadistic public school he'd attended. She'd wept and raged until Pa agreed that Alfie could attend King Henry's College in Kings Lynn as a weekly boarder, so she could have him home every weekend.

Now Pa stayed in London most of the time, running an investment company, and Alfie and Ma lived in Wrigton Hall, the family home, a drafty Georgian house a mile or so from Wells, with a cluster of holiday cottages converted from stables and cowsheds. Alfie suspected that Pa was shacked up with a younger floozy in their handsome Hampstead flat, but that subject was never broached with Ma.

'I'll just put the tray down here, shall I?' said Ma. 'I know how you love your Florentines.'

Alfie gritted his teeth. 'Yes, that'll be fine.' Then, after a pause. 'Thanks.'

He waited for her to go, but she hovered there, obviously with something more to say. 'Are you sure you're OK to drive, darling?'

'Of course I'm OK,' he snapped, turning round to glare at her. What was she fussing about? He'd only had a couple of glasses of red with lunch.

'If you say so.' She took a couple of short, noisy breaths. 'What time will you be back? I'll rustle up some supper.'

Alfie licked dry lips – food was the last thing on his mind – and steeled himself to be pleasant. 'I'm not sure when we'll finish Ma. No need to wait up.'

'If you say so. Only I really think you should eat more than you do. Just look at you – there's nothing of you.'

'I'm fine, Ma,' he said, leaning towards the mirror again, willing her to leave. Eventually, with an audible sigh, Ma turned and headed out of the room, shutting the door loudly behind her. 'Why can't you leave me alone?' muttered Alfie, as her footsteps clomped downstairs. For many years Alfie had felt sorry for his sister, but the last time they'd met up, in some rowdy bar in Shoreditch, she'd been blissfully happy on the arm of a handsome, butch woman with a crew cut, and had dished out a few words of advice for him.

'You need to get out,' she'd said, while the GF stroked her thigh. 'Ma'll eat you alive if you stay there much longer.'

He'd blustered and joked but it had hit a sore spot. Face it: he was nearly 30 (though he only owned up to 27) and a mummy's boy. He'd never been to university – couldn't be arsed to work for the grades – and never lived away from home. The holiday cottages had kept him busy for the past decade, but he was bored with that now. Bored, bored, bored with people moaning about a scratch on the fridge or a stain on the sofa. Bored with charming the pants off women in baggy linen smocks and uptight men escaping from their pressured city lives. He particularly hated the spoilt brats who scribbled on the furniture with felt-tip pens – scribbles *he* had to erase since the cleaner only managed to make them worse when she went at them with bleach and solvent.

But he had a foolproof plan to get out: it would be bye bye holiday cottages once he'd scored himself a role in a film. Look at all those posh boys who'd made stellar careers for themselves: Alfie was every bit as good-looking as they were. An old pal from school was planning to make a film set in the 1950s about a British public school boy who gets dragged into the crazy Soho scene of sleazy bars, uppers and downers. He'd as good as said the role was Alfie's. He just needed to see him act.

And that meant persuading Hengist to give him the part of Bertie Wooster.

* *

Janette Tinker

Janette Tinker sat in the bay window of The Globe, waiting for her boyfriend Jem to return from the bar. He'd texted her from the pub and she'd agreed to meet him for a quick drink before setting off for the auditions of *Jeeves Pulls it Off*.

'You know what?' said Jem in a loud, boastful voice, returning with the drinks, 'You're bloody gorgeous.'

'Shhh! Everyone'll hear you.' She glanced around, but only one other table was occupied, by a group of lads talking loudly about the fate of Norwich City.

After putting the drinks down (mineral water for her, and a pint – his second – for him) Jem slung his burly arm round her shoulders sending his smell of sawdust up her nose. 'I don't care. I bloody love you. You know that, don't you?'

Despite wishing he'd stop shouting, despite the fact that it probably hadn't been the brightest idea to meet him before the auditions, Janette felt a smile creep over her face. Jem loved her. He'd do anything for her. Anything. And look at him: a six-foot-four carpenter, with muscles hard as tennis balls.

The trouble was he didn't understand that she had to keep in Hengist's good books if she was to be cast as Madeline Bassett. She *needed* that part. She was already 20 years old, and determined to make progress with her acting career. And Hengist had promised to get an agent he knew to come and see her. She knew she'd be signed up as soon as she was seen.

But first she had to do Hengist a little favour. Nothing

too serious. Then she'd be cast in the role of Madeline Basset, and her acting career could properly take off. Because she *knew* she had talent – knew it in her guts. Apart from anything else, she'd outshone everyone else in every production she'd taken part in. When she was sixteen, her teenage drama club in Sheringham had put on a production of *Cabaret*. She'd played Sally Bowles, and had brought the house down every night.

It was just a shame that the audience consisted mainly of parents and siblings who whined and fidgeted all the way through.

Her mum'd be waiting up for her after the auditions, even though she was doing a double shift at the nursing home today, shifting old ladies on and off their commodes. Janette sighed. Her mum was one of those poor sods who were going to have to work until they dropped because the pension age for women had gone up. She was 63 now: Janette had been an unexpected arrival when she was in her forties. Bunions, bad knees, heartburn: you name it, her mum had it.

Which was why Janette was going to make it big. She was going to be a successful actor if it killed her. Her mum would be so proud of her. All those years of scrimping and saving, of taking her to drama classes, talent shows, festivals – they'd be worth it when she saw Janette in the role of Madeline Bassett in *Jeeves Pulls it Off*.

There was no way she or her mum could afford to pay for drama school, and she didn't want to rack up huge debts, so she was going to have to work her way up – not like those public-school twats who walked into the best parts because they knew the right people and went to RADA. Others had done it: look at Sheridan Smith. She hadn't been born with a silver spoon in her mouth. She hadn't been to drama school. Besides, the artistic director of the National Youth

Theatre had said that drama schools were a waste of time and money. All you needed was talent and determination. She fancied herself in *Les Miserables*, starting in the chorus and then ...

Her phone pinged, bringing her back down to earth from her visions of success on the West End stage. Her heart gave an almighty thump as she read the text: Hengist wanted to have a private word with her before the auditions.

Thank goodness Jem had gone to the bogs. If he saw the text he'd go into one of his moods.

But despite Jem's sulks, she was going to strike a deal with Hengist.

Yes she *was*.

* *

Cedric Williams

Hearing the back door open, Cedric Williams rapidly pressed Send and slipped his phone into his jacket pocket. Standing up, he surveyed himself in the full-length mirror on the bedroom wall of his comfortable home on the outskirts of Wells: grubby jeans, a shapeless old denim jacket, trainers that had seen better days. His hair could do with a cut, too: grey wisps dribbling over his collar, bald patch shining in the sun beaming in the bedroom window. Perhaps Hengist would have second thoughts about casting him as the immaculate Jeeves while he looked like this.

Hearing footsteps running up the stairs he hastily sat down again. The door opened and his wife Sheila blundered in, grinning, her broad face shining with sweat from her jog with Thatcher, their golden retriever.

'Hello darling,' she said, bounding over and kissing him on the cheek, expelling a blast of stale, coffee-infused breath. 'Thought I'd come back early to wish you luck at the auditions tonight. Not that you need it: you're a shoo-in for the role of Jeeves.'

Cedric forced himself to smile. 'Oh, I don't know. Perhaps Hengist has someone else in mind. He's always saying we should bring in new blood.'

'Don't be daft. You're the star of the company. You know that.'

'There are plenty of people younger and more handsome than me.'

'Yes, but you can *act*, darling,' she said, treating him to another noisy smacker. 'Anyway, I'm going to have a shower. If I don't see you before you leave, break a leg.'

And with that, she bounced out of the door. Cedric watched her go with a sinking feeling in the pit of his belly. Sheila had been an excellent mother to their two girls (both settled in London, carving careers for themselves in the media), and an extremely capable wife who'd taken care of the running of the house, leaving him free to pursue his career as an editor of a weekly literary magazine, working in London four days a week. When the girls left home, she converted their spare garage into a studio apartment and embarked on high-end B and B which, due to her excellent marketing and management, pulled in enough money to allow him to leave his job with a handsome redundancy package, and pursue his dream as a writer. In the past decade he'd published four modestly successful non-fiction books about artistic movements.

Thank heavens he had to go to London frequently to research them.

When they were first married he'd admired Sheila's relentless energy and positivity, though their relationship had never scaled the heights of passion. He'd been proud of her when she was elected to the local council as an independent. But in the past few years she'd shifted further and further to the right. She now felt it was her duty to pronounce on 'family values'. She thought gay marriage was ridiculous, and opposed the rights of gay people to adopt, saying they couldn't possibly offer a child the stability of a normal family. She was also a great fan of austerity, saying to all and sundry that we had to be unselfish and put our country first.

When she first spouted these opinions, he'd argued with her, but he'd learned that nothing he said made any difference. With a tolerant smile she'd pretend to listen, then shake her head and tell him he was naive. 'You've got your head in the clouds, darling. You're a dear, creative soul, but you're completely impractical. Where on earth would you be without me to look after you?'

Thinking of those words now, his cheeks burned. It was humiliating to be patronised, to be patted on the head like a child.

Feeling his phone vibrate, he pulled it out of his pocket. As he read the screen a shudder ran through him.

What had he got himself into?

3

In which Rags meets The Peasmarsh Players

By early evening clouds had blown in from the North Sea, taking the place of the sunny warmth of the morning.

I ran myself a bath and, since there was no shower in the flat, wrestled a newly purchased rubber hose over the hot and cold taps so I could wash my hair. Then I sank under the surface of the cooling water, because to sit up gave me goose pimples. Before I turned into a prune I pulled myself out of the bath, wrapped myself in a towel and retreated to the bedroom, where an electric two-bar fire was fighting with the breeze whistling through a crack in one of the sash windows.

I pulled on a pair of faded jeans and a funky embroidered blouse I'd picked up in a Fakenham charity shop. Pale green, embroidered with flowers and leaves, it complemented the colour of my hair, which had picked up a few blonde highlights during my time in the south of France. I dried my hair, grabbed a cotton jumper, and headed out to the not-so-mean streets of Wells-next-the-Sea.

Dad and Susie picked me up at The Buttlands and we headed to Peasmarsh, a village a mile and a half away, where The Peasmarsh Players were meeting up in the Coach and Horses. As we drove, Dad explained that the company rehearsed in the church hall. 'And the Coach and Horses is never too busy – not like Wells at holiday times – and convenient if people want to have a bite to eat before rehearsals.'

Peasmarsh was one of those sleepy Norfolk villages enriched by the wool trade, boasting an imposing, flint-faced church (St Botolph's), a scatter of red-roofed cottages, and some bland new-build housing.

I liked the Coach and Horses – a large, rambling pub that still retained some old wooden benches and booths, and a cosy snug. The Peasmarsh Players were gathered in the main bar, beneath sepia photographs and faded prints of agricultural workers and fishing boats. As soon as we'd bought our drinks and found somewhere to sit, Dad introduced me to a young man with angular features and jet black hair sitting at an adjacent table. 'This is Alfie, who's hoping to be our Bertie Wooster.' I nodded and said hello: he flashed me a toothy smile. Long-limbed and undeniably suave in a loose linen jacket and Oxford bags, he seemed a little tense – probably pre-audition nerves. Before we had a chance to chat, his phone rang and with a muttered apology he turned away to take the call.

A young woman with a gleaming tumble of blonde hair hurried over, looking for a seat as the pub filled up.

'Can I join you?' she asked.

Susie invited her to sit down. 'This is Janette, another one of the Players. Janette, this is Rags, Graham's daughter. She's just moved to Wells and is thinking of getting involved with the company.'

Janette held out a hand. 'Hi. Good to meet you. If you

want to know anything about Wells, just ask. I've lived there all my life.'

I liked her immediately, and not just because of her Norfolk accent, which, like my dad's, added a lazy lilt to her words. Her handshake was firm – I can't stand women who offer a limp, floppy grip – and there was a bright intelligence in her eyes. She was dressed in shorts and dark tights which showed off her long, shapely legs.

'That's Betzy, who's playing Aunt Agatha,' she said, pointing to a woman with a severe face queuing at the bar. Oh, and that's Toots, our wardrobe mistress. She's a real character.'

She looked it. Toots was plump – gloriously so – with a cleavage trying to burst free of a teal silk blouse. Her legs were encased in what used to be called 'slacks' – cream cotton trousers that tapered from her shapely backside to her ankles. Her shoes were red leather pumps that hadn't come from Matalan. As I watched, she exchanged a few words with the spotty youth serving behind the bar and burst into loud laughter, throwing her head back so that her thick auburn hair rippled down her back. I found myself smiling: she looked like she'd be a lot of fun to hang out with.

'Dave, over there,' said Susie, pointing out a solid young man with pale hair sipping a pint of bitter, 'he's hoping to be cast as Gussy Fink-Nottle.'

Feeling our gaze upon him, Dave turned and smiled at us. Though not handsome, he had an open, agreeable face that made me warm to him.

'Oh, and that's Hengist Bright, our director,' said Susie, nodding towards a slender dude with a silky grey ponytail and a black eye patch who'd just entered the pub.

I watched him with interest. He was a hawkish, good-looking man of around fifty, with an air of arrogance, but undeniable charisma. When Dad and Susie went to talk to a couple of friends at the bar, I couldn't resist asking Janette if she knew how he got the eye patch.

'A childhood accident, I think. I'm so used to it I don't notice it any more.'

'And what's he like to work with?'

She flashed a brief, bright smile. 'Oh, he's the most fantastic director. And because he doesn't need to work – his wife, Mindy, is loaded – he can put all his energy into the company.'

Though her voice was cheerful, I detected a wistful note of envy that suggested she had to work for every penny that came her way. Her clothes, though funky, were clearly not new.

'How long have you been involved with the Players?'

'A couple of years – since I left school. It's all I want to do – act. And if Hengist casts me as Madeline Bassett, I can get an agent to come and see me.'

'Have you got much competition?'

She shrugged and swept her hair off her face. 'A couple of other girls are interested, but I know I'm the best person for the role.'

'Well, good luck. I'm sure you'd be terrific.' I pointed at Alfie, now lounging at the bar, showing off his best profile. 'My dad told me Alfie's likely to be Bertie Wooster. He looks the part, doesn't he?'

She laughed. 'He certainly does.'

I offered to buy her a drink – an offer she gratefully accepted. At the bar Susie introduced me to Toots, who was working her way through a large glass of red.

'Toots Riley,' she said, holding out her hand for me to shake. 'Are you going to try for a part?'

'No way, but I'm happy to help with the costumes. I'm crap at sewing but pretty good at finding bargains in charity shops.'

She threw her head back and did that big laugh again. 'You sound perfect, darling. Do you fancy coming round for a coffee one morning, and we'll map out a plan of action?'

'I'd love that.'

At that moment Dad tapped me on the arm and asked me if I'd be OK to make my own way back to Wells, because Susie needed to get back to Cromer to pick up Cocoa, her Labradoodle, from the vet's surgery, where she'd been having a minor operation.

'Susie'd like me to go with her,' he added. 'You don't mind, do you?'

'Of course not.'

'I'll look after Rags,' said Toots, overhearing our conversation. 'You get on.'

Thanking her, Dad and Susie downed the last of their drinks and headed for the door.

At ten to eight we decamped to the church hall, a flint-faced building adjacent to St Botolph's churchyard. I'd expected a musty, fusty place, but the hall was clean and bright, with swish red velvet curtains adorning the stage. Tall windows gave sweeping views across heath land to the coast, and a well equipped kitchen to the left of the front door opened on to a serving hatch on which soft drinks were laid out.

I grabbed myself a glass of mineral water and took a seat next to Toots.

At eight on the dot Hengist started to man-splain arrangements for the production. Janette was sitting close to him, her hair now clipped back in a way that showed off the sharp planes of her face. Alfie was fidgeting on a chair on the other side of the circle. Betzy, (cast as the bossy Aunt Agatha), sat there looking bored, and the circle was completed by a few other men and women in their thirties and forties who'd been at the pub. Sitting close to Hengist was a young man I hadn't seen before – lanky, with light brown hair and a scrubby beard. Dressed in a scruffy jumper and jeans, he was slouched in his chair, yawning conspicuously now and then.

After Hengist had informed us that the play was to be put on in the snazzy Wells Maltings in December, he moved on to talk about the casting process. 'Some parts have already been cast, but tonight I shall be doing my utmost to find the remaining actors who can realise my vision for this production. In particular, it's imperative I cast *la crème de la crème* in the leading roles,' he intoned. 'That's why I'll be weighing my decisions with the utmost care. Nothing must be left to chance. Nothing.'

'Is he always like this?' I whispered to Toots.

'Yes. Plus, the production is being entered into a regional competition for amateur productions. We've come second for the last three years, so he's got a giant bee in his bonnet about winning this time.'

Hengist wound up his motivational speech by announcing that he'd already decided that 'the very talented Cedric Williams will be perfect in the part of Jeeves.' A solid man in grubby jeans stood up and took a mock bow. He looked about as suited to take the role of Jeeves as I was to play Hamlet, but Toots confirmed in my ear that he was the best actor in the company by a long chalk, and always landed the lead roles.

'And tonight I hope to find my Bertie Wooster and Madeline Bassett. Wish me god speed,' concluded Hengist, his voice rising to a dramatic climax.

Toots and I exchanged raised eyebrows.

'And now it's time to talk about costumes and sets,' Hengist continued, voice dropping to a more mundane level, 'as everything must be of the highest quality. Everything.'

A wiry woman with jet black hair cut into an asymmetrical

bob cleared her throat and took over.

'That's Mindy, his wife,' whispered Toots. 'The brains behind the operation. A real power house.'

After a crisp introduction, Mindy handed round some perfectly typed sheets. One gave a rehearsal schedule, starting the following week. The second set out the technical requirements, including lists of costumes and props required. Toots scanned the costume list and nodded. 'As usual she's got it all covered, down to the smallest detail. I mean, look at this: 'One blue and white spotted handkerchief approximately 30 cm square.'

'What happens if you can't get what she lists?'

'That never happens. We order things online if we can't buy them locally.'

'Any questions?' said Mindy, in a penetrating voice that showed she was used to being listened to.

A meek silence followed before Hengist spoke up again.

'I sincerely hope the casting will be concluded tonight, but, as I've already said, I'm not prepared to settle for second best. If I have to call another casting session in the next few days, so be it.'

I wasn't surprised to see Alfie's jaw tense up: Hengist was behaving as if he were casting a Hollywood blockbuster rather than The Peasmarsh Players' production of *Jeeves Pulls it Off.*

'Thank you everyone,' said Hengist. 'Those auditioning, please stay behind. The rest of you are free to go.'

Toots and I walked back to Wells along the quiet lanes, and settled ourselves in The Eddie (The Edinburgh) so we could chat about the costumes. She explained that the Players had a modest costume store, housed in her box room, and ticked off items such as shirts she knew were already there. We agreed that things such as blazers and flapper dresses could probably be sourced at charity shops or online, though we'd have to make a few alterations.

I reminded her that sewing wasn't my strong suit, but she said that didn't matter. 'We'll go shopping together then I can handle all the stuff with needle and thread. We've got a budget of £400; that should be enough. And if we're really stuck, Mindy will find some more cash. Her family have lived here for generations and she knows who to tap for funds. Plus I'm sure she digs into her own pocket now and then – and they're deep pockets.'

'What does she do?'

'She's some sort of financial consultant for IT start ups, and is always whizzing off to other countries to advise organisations on how to launch their projects.' She leaned a little closer. 'Her father died recently, and she came into a shed-load of money. She and Hengist are planning to convert a barn further along the coast into a permanent home for the company and a venue for touring productions.'

'Wow. That's a big project.'

'It's his dream, and she'll do anything to make him happy.'

We started to exchange life stories. With my tongue relaxed by wine and good company I found myself telling her about my family – about how much I loved my dad, and how happy I was that our relationship was repaired. Then I moved on to the topic of my mother, Gwendolyn. 'I know I should say she's my best friend, blah, blah,' I said, 'but we've never been close and I find her ...' I paused, searching for a word that didn't make me sound like a monster, '... challenging.'

Toots gave me a frank, searching look. 'You mean she drives you nuts.'

'Something like that.'

'You're not alone, my darling,' said Toots, picking up on the guilt creeping into my voice. 'My relationship with my mother's pretty crap, too. I'm an only child, and for as long as I can remember she's competed with me. When I was a teenager she flirted with all my boyfriends. She even had an affair with one of them! And whenever I had a party, she insisted on being there and showing off – boasting about all the men who fancied her. It was toe-curling.'

'What about your dad?'

'He scarpered when I was five. Set up home with a lovely, no-nonsense woman called Pat and had another five children. The weekends I spent with them were the happiest times in my childhood, though they never had two pennies to rub together.' She gave me a sad smile. 'My mother's lost most of her marbles and is living in a posh care home in Hove, still announcing to all and sundry that the three male residents want to get into her knickers.'

'Sounds grim.'

'It's not so bad. Ma's being well looked after, and she doesn't miss me. She can't remember who I am most of the time. And I have five wonderful stepsisters and brothers and am an auntie to goodness knows how many children.' She beamed. 'I couldn't be happier.'

Wishing I had a disposition as sunny as hers, I made my way to the bar to buy us both another drink. There I was surprised to run into Janette Tinker.

'That didn't take long,' I said. 'Did the casting finish early?'

'No. They'll be there for a while, but Hengist cast Madeline Bassett first.' Her smile lit up like a flashbulb. 'He told me no one else was remotely suited to the part and that it was mine.' She turned to a beefy young man standing beside her, gazing at her with undisguised adoration. 'And this is Jem, my boyfriend.' She jabbed him in the ribs. 'Say hello to Rags, Jem.'

Reluctantly he pulled his gaze away from Janette's beautiful breasts and turned towards me, holding out a tanned hand. 'Hi. How are you doing?'

I shook his hand. Though not as stunning as Janette, he was a good-looking lad with even features and shiny, dark brown hair clipped short at the back of a suntanned neck. 'Good to meet you. I've just moved to Wells.'

He pulled a business card out of his pocket, on which was printed his name, and a hammer and saw. 'Let me know if you need any carpentry work doing. I've got my own business, and I'll give you a good price: any friend of Janette is a friend of mine,' he said, in the blurred, careful way people speak when they've been drinking for a while.

'So did you have any competition for the part?' I asked Janette.

She beamed. 'A couple of other girls auditioned, but I always knew I was right it.'And what about Bertie Wooster? Did Alfie get the part?'

'I don't know. Hengist was still seeing people when I left.'

With a little wave of her fingers, Janette said farewell and led Jem to a small table, where he slung his arm round her shoulders. I bought two more glasses of Merlot and returned to Toots. We chatted easily, exchanging tales of love, life and everything else until nearly midnight.

I rolled home pleasantly merry, pleased to have made a new friend in Toots.

4

In which Rags gets asked to do a favour for an old enemy

I was woken just after eight by the ringing of my phone. Groggy, I grabbed for it. As soon as I picked up, a loud voice leapt from the handset: 'It's Tracey. I need to talk to you.'

I sat up straight. 'Why? What's happened?' Tracey Jones, a young mother of two hyperactive boys who lived close to my dad in Fakenham, wasn't my biggest fan, so I couldn't imagine why she was calling me.

'My best friend Zillah's been questioned by the police. They think she attacked someone, but she never did.'

'Who? Who do they think she's attacked?'

'Some old man. A vicar. They've been asking Zillah all these questions, and she rang me in a right old state and the only person I could think of was you. So will you help, or not?'

I struggled into a sitting position. 'Slow down a bit. Tell me who's been attacked.'

'That trendy vicar at Peasmarsh. The one with a ponytail.'

'When?'

'Last night. Someone found him in St Botolph's churchyard first thing.'

I thought back for a moment: The Peasmarsh Players parked their cars on the street outside the church, so surely someone would have seen something if the vicar was attacked before they went home. He must have come to grief later on.

Tracey cut into my thoughts by taking a big breath and yelling, 'So will you come over?'

I considered her request for a few seconds: Tracey was broke, and her friend was probably in the same boat. On the other hand, since leaving the dog-eat-dog media scrum of London I'd resolved to be more generous.

'I'll be there as soon as I can.'

I made myself a coffee and a slice of toast then set off.

The sun was gilding the fields as I pootled up the dry road (so-called because there's no pub along its nine miles) towards Fakenham. I loved North Norfolk. I loved the quiet roads, the tawny marsh harriers that hunted on the Holkham Estate, the markets crammed with bric-a-brac and fresh vegetables.

And I loved being closer to Dad. We'd been virtually estranged when I turned up at his house in June. Since then we'd had our ups and downs, but we were on the way to having a proper dad-daughter relationship.

Tracey was waiting for me as I turned into The Terrace, wearing her usual outfit of outsize tee-shirt and leggings which barely contained her sizable arse. 'You took your time!' she barked.

Gritting my teeth, I squeezed my car into a tiny space.

'The kids are out,' she threw over her shoulder, as she marched ahead of me up the road and round to the path that ran between the back yards and gardens of The Terrace. 'My mum's looking after them. But they'll be back in ten minutes, so we haven't got long.'

A few moments later we were sitting in her kitchen, where dirty crockery was piled on the draining board and in the sink. No change there, then. Tracey didn't offer me tea or coffee and though I thought of asking for a glass of water, the glitter of tears in her eyes stopped me. This was a Tracey I hadn't seen before.

'Tell me what's happened.'

'Zillah's been staying in a flat attached to the church, and this morning the police came and banged on her door and questioned her for ages. She's totally freaked out. We've got to help her.'

'And you say they suspect her of attacking the vicar?'

Tracey's shoulders lifted then fell in a huge shrug that released a whiff of sweat and fried food. 'Some busybody told the police they heard her arguing with the vicar yesterday, but she told me they get on really well – that he's a great bloke.' Her face filled with fierce determination. 'Why would she attack him? I won't let them put her away for something she never did. I bloody *won't*!'

'Why don't you give me some background? Tell me about Zillah.'

It emerged that Zillah and Tracey had been inseparable at primary school. 'She was really sweet to me when the other kids called me fatty and lard-arse. We both had single mums – my dad had buggered off and hers had died when she was a baby.' Tracey's eyes narrowed. 'But everything changed when we were in our last year of primary school. Her mum won a big prize on the lottery and they moved to Norwich. For a while we stayed in touch and she came and visited during the summer holidays when it was the Wells carnival.' Her face softened. 'We went crabbing – one year we won the prize for catching the most crabs. Or we'd get the little steam train to the beach. She used to pay for our tickets out of her pocket money, because Mum was always skint,' she added, her dreamy expression giving me a glimpse of the girl she'd been before she had two small sons driving her round the twist. She jumped up and rooted around in a drawer full of papers until she found what she wanted. 'Here.'

She thrust a photograph of a girl of about 15 with pale auburn hair and a distinctive, narrow face under my nose. I studied it for a few moments, then took a photograph of it with my phone.

'Anyway, her mum got involved with some stupid religious cult called The Sistren – one of those that won't let you have operations and stuff like that – and Zillah stopped coming to see me. Neither of us had mobiles back then, so that was it. We lost touch. But then she called me out of the blue saying she'd left the religious nutters and was staying at the church in Peasmarsh.'

'How long's she been here?'

'A couple of months. Her mum's been looking for her, but Zillah made me swear not to tell anyone, so when her mum found my number and rang me I pretended I hadn't got a clue where she was.'

'And when did you last see her?'

'She came over about three weeks ago. Said she had something special to tell me. But I didn't have time to talk to her properly because Roddy was throwing up all over the place, and Damon broke something and I got into a strop and ...'

Instead of finishing her sentence she gave another of her huge shrugs, but she didn't need to say more. I could guess what had happened: Tracey had lost her rag, and Zillah had given up on the visit.

'So, will you talk to her?' she barked.

'Give me her number.'

As Tracey read it out, the sounds of a baby bawling and yells of, 'No! No!' signalled the return of her two kids. Wearily, Tracey stood up and went to the back door. Her mum – a carbon copy of Tracey, but with a gentler face – extracted a scarlet-faced Roddy from his buggy and handed him over. 'Here you are, Trace. I'm afraid he needs a change.'

Damon had stopped dead and was staring at me, silent for once. I bent down to his level and winked. 'Hello there, Damon.'

He stuck his thumb in his mouth and kept sizing me up. Some time ago I'd offered to take him out for the day to Wells but since then I'd been busy and hadn't got it together. Tracey had been glowering at me ever since, and I didn't blame her. I made a mental note to deliver on the offer as soon as I could.

Damon barged past me and started tugging at Tracey's tee-shirt shouting, 'Me want sweets!'

With a hasty goodbye, I left.

I rang Zillah as soon as I was out of the house. She didn't pick up, so I left a message. Normally I'd have dropped in on Dad but he was at Susie's for a couple of days, helping her with some decorating while caring for the convalescing Cocoa, so I returned to my car and headed back to the coast.

As I drove I searched my memory: I was sure I'd seen her – or someone who looked very like the photograph of her – recently.

Then it came to me. She'd been sitting at a table outside The Bowling Green pub a couple of weeks ago, with a glass of water in front of her. Something about her manner had told me she was waiting for someone.

Someone she was longing to see.

5

In which we meet the ethereal Zillah

By the time I got back to Wells, Zillah had left me a message, saying she was in one of the seafront cafes. I hurried down there.

Zillah Lloyd had the narrow, ascetic face of a medieval saint, with creamy skin and hair that hovered between blonde and auburn. She was sitting cross-legged on a sofa, hands clasped tightly around a mug of peppermint tea. A gold cross hung round her neck, glowing against her pale skin. Dressed in baggy linen trousers, Ugg boots, and a loose cotton shirt, she exuded the sort of shabby chic reality TV stars spend a fortune to achieve.

'Thank you for agreeing to see me.'

'It's my pleasure. I only live up the road,' I said making a vague gesture towards Staithe Street. 'I fancied a coffee and a bite to eat in any case.'

Her worried grey eyes locked on to mine. 'You probably think I'm being pathetic, but being questioned by the police really freaked me out.'

'It's scary but not unusual in the circumstances,' I said, making my voice as soothing as possible. 'When someone sustains a serious injury, they'll talk to people who were nearby to try to find out whether any crime was involved.'

'So am I a suspect?'

'Have they cautioned you?'

'No.'

'Or told you they'll want to speak to you again?'

'No.'

'Then it seems highly unlikely.'

She gave me a shy smile. 'Thank you.'

'Were you on good terms with Reverend Blackthorn?' I asked, feeling I should probe a little more deeply, in case there was anything in their relationship that might be deemed suspicious by the police.

'Yes. More than good terms. Hugh was my saviour.' She closed long fingers around the cross hanging round her neck. 'He took me in when I needed sanctuary. I would never harm him. *Never.*'

'So you hadn't argued or anything?'

She hesitated. 'No. Never. Well hardly ever.'

I raised my eyebrows a fraction.

Her fingers tightened on the crucifix. 'Once or twice he challenged me about staying in The Sistren for so long. About wasting my life – that sort of thing. But he always came round and apologised afterwards.'

'And you didn't see or hear anything unusual on the night he was injured?'

'No. I was in my flat, reading, and went to bed early.' Tears filled her eyes. 'And now he's in hospital. They took him away in an ambulance.'

'I'm sure he'll be getting excellent care. Try not to worry.'

We sat in silence for a few minutes. I took a bite of my gooey chocolate brownie while Zillah sipped her tea.

'They won't come round to my flat again, will they?'

'I don't think so.'

She put down her mug, looking at me with worry in her eyes. 'There have been people hanging around the church all morning. A reporter rang the bell and looked through the window at me. It was horrible.'

'You didn't open the door, did you?'

'No. But you've got to understand, I don't want any publicity. If my mother finds out where I am she'll try to drag me back to The Sistren house. Tracey told you about them, didn't she?'

I nodded.

'And I won't let her do that to me.' She took a few deep breaths. 'Sorry. I'm a bit anxious at the moment.'

'It's OK. I understand. Just keep a low profile and don't answer the door or the phone to anyone unless you're sure you know them. The press and social media will soon move on to something else.'

'Thanks.' She gave me another shy smile that illumined her face. I sipped my excellent espresso, hoping I'd put her mind at rest. What a strange fish she was: not pretty, but verging on beautiful when her face relaxed. Shy but courageous – it couldn't have been easy to leave a cult like The Sistren – and resourceful.

'So how come you went to St Botolph's?'

A faint pink tinted Zillah's cheeks. 'I found a letter from Hugh – Reverend Blackthorn – in Mum's secret box – the one she kept under her bed. She'd left it unlocked after she got out her passport because she's planning a trip to Lourdes. I know I shouldn't have been looking through her things, but I was desperate to leave The Sistren and I thought maybe I could find a relative who'd take me in. I came across a letter from Hugh to Mum, sent about ten years ago. He said that if she ever needed help, she should get in touch, and at the end he'd added, *The same goes for Zillah.*

'The letter was from a theology college. So I rang them. They said they couldn't give out any personal information, but I gathered from our conversation that Hugh had been training to be a minister. So I googled him and found out he was the vicar of St Botolph's. When I rang he was so kind, so generous. He told me I could come and stay in the church as long as I liked.' Tears welled up in her eyes. 'And now he's in hospital, fighting for his life.'

I pulled a clean cotton handkerchief from my pocket – something I'd learned from Dad is always a great comfort. With muttered thanks she took it, blotted her eyes and blew her nose.

'I just hope he'll be OK,' she mumbled. 'He's a good man through and through. I can talk to him about anything, and his parishioners adore him. I always go to his services. You see, though I've left The Sistren I still believe in the grace of God. Meeting Hugh – staying at the church – was a dream come true.'

'What prompted you to finally make the break from The Sistren?'

'A new sister joined us about a year ago – Sister Deirdre – and she was amazing. She thought we should be trying to make a difference – to be out there in the world – and was working with a charity that helps the homeless. Plus she played secular music, though she wasn't really supposed to. We'd spend hours in her room listening to people like Marvin Gaye on headphones, so no one else could hear. It got me all … all churned up.'

I bet it did, I thought, remembering Marvin's classic album *Let's Get it On*, which extols the pleasures of sex between consenting anybodies.

'And Deirdre said it was wrong to keep me cooped up in The Sistren house. She persuaded Mother Paul Marie, the head of our community, to let me join her when she went on night patrols round Norwich, taking food and blankets to the homeless.'

'What was that like?'

Zillah's face lit up. 'Amazing. We didn't just hand out stuff: we talked to them, told them where to get help if they wanted it. The charity we worked with made me feel I was doing something worthwhile. It was like I'd been in a giant freezer and suddenly I was melting.'

She looked down into her mug, then back at me, with shining eyes. 'It was exciting, but scary. Very scary. My mother didn't approve.' Zillah's face hardened. 'She's a fanatic: she even changed her name from Julie to Julian, in honour of Saint Julian of Norwich. And when she found out Deirdre had been playing me secular music she went berserk, yelling that she was a bad influence, leading me into the ways of evil. For once I argued back, so she went to Mother Paul Marie and got Deirdre chucked out of The Sistren. I'll *never* forgive her for that. Never. I *hate* her.'

The ferocity in Zillah's voice made me look at her again. So she wasn't all Christian charity, sweetness and light.

'And when Deirdre went, I decided I had to get out.'

'Did you keep in touch with her?'

Zillah sighed. 'I wish. I don't know where she is. I mean, where do you start? I don't even know her surname.'

'That's a shame.'

We sat for a few moments amidst the cheerful clatter of the cafe.

Sitting up straighter, she pushed a strand of red-gold hair back from her face. 'But I did it. I left The Sistren.'

'Good for you.'

'I'm paying rent, you know,' she said. 'I've got money. I found a big pile of cash in Mum's box and borrowed enough to tide me over for a few months.' She gave me a look containing a pinch of mischief. 'I know I shouldn't have taken it, but I'll pay her back. I'm going to find myself a job and get my life sorted out.' She drained the last of her peppermint tea. 'But I don't want her knowing where I am. Not yet.'

'Tracey's worried about you.'

'I know, and I'm grateful. She's been a good friend. We bonded when we were at primary school 'cos we were both misfits. My mum was depressed. Hers was done for shop lifting.'

Ah. That explained Tracey's sensitivity to police investigations. 'That must have been hard for her.'

'It was. We stuck up for each other. It was us against the bullies. I was gutted when my mum dragged me off to Norwich. Then we moved into The Sistren house, and that was the end of my trips to the coast.' Her face tightened into a frown. 'She didn't want me in the company of sinners and non-believers.'

At this point my phone pinged. I pulled it out to find a text saying that a BT Openworld engineer could come to my flat some time after one o'clock.

'Is there anything else you want to discuss with me?' I asked, 'only I've just heard that an engineer is coming to set up my broadband this afternoon.'

She shook her head. 'I'm good, thanks. You get off.'

'You've got my number, haven't you? You can ring me any time.'

She held up her phone. 'I saved it when you rang me earlier on. And thanks again.'

Did BT Openworld turn up? Of course not. I mooched around the flat for five hours, cleaning dusty kitchen cupboards and rearranging the few pieces of crockery I'd picked up at Fakenham market. I rang Carola, my oldest friend, suggesting I pay a brief visit to collect the stuff I'd stored in her basement when I left London. She didn't pick up – she's a solicitor with three huge sons and a busy schedule – so I left her a message. 'Or you could come and see me,' I added at the end, because in truth I didn't have a burning desire to visit London. In fact I had no desire at all. A small part of me was scared that I'd run into the blood-sucking landlord who'd doubled my rent within two years. Though I'd arranged a schedule of payments to deal with the rent arrears I owed, I had visions of him haranguing me all the way down Stoke Newington Church Street.

Once I'd done all the tidying and rearranging I could, I settled in to wait for the elusive engineer, twitching the curtains of the window overlooking Staithe Street, in case I hadn't heard the wheezy doorbell.

When I finally cracked and rang a harassed person in a call centre she checked and said that the engineer had been held up on a complicated job. Muttering curses I stalked around the flat, kicking a few cushions on the way. Just before five I got a text saying the appointment would be rescheduled.

I swore loudly (again) and pulled a bottle of wine out of the fridge, settling down to another night with my DVDs – no great hardship, as I was working through the stack which I'd abandoned when I signed up for Netflix. I settled on the pleasures of *Atonement* (I'm a sucker for a good WW2 movie) and *Trading Places*. Yes, I'd watched it at least half a dozen times, but Eddie Murphy still had me laughing out loud.

I had an early night and slept in. I surfaced around eight, made myself a strong espresso, warmed a croissant, and was tucking into its buttery flakes when my phone rang.

Tracey.

'It's Zillah,' she yelled. 'She's *disappeared.*'

6

In which Rags is offered the chance to earn some money

Gulping, snuffling, Tracey filled me in. 'My friend Lisa, who works in the Wells Co-op, overheard that old bag of a parish secretary telling someone she found Zillah's door wide open and everything smashed up.'

'That's terrible.'

'I *knew* she was in danger. I just knew it.' Tracey's worried breaths rushed out of the phone. 'What shall we do?'

'I'll go up to the church – see if I can find out any more.'

By the time I arrived at St Botolph's word about the break-in had clearly got round, because a clump of a dozen or so people, some with dogs, were clustered around the side of the church. I strolled over, hoping to get a peek into the flat at the side of the church where she'd been staying.

But that area had been fenced off with yellow police incident tape, and a young female police officer stood on the path, making sure no one went too close. On tiptoe,

I could just about make out two figures moving around behind the leaded-light windows.

'Disgusting, isn't it?' said an elderly woman standing nearby. 'It's something when you can't even be safe in a church.'

'I don't know what things are coming to,' said her companion, a diminutive man. 'First the reverend and now this girl. It's a blooming disgrace.'

I edged closer.

The woman was nodding in agreement. 'There could be a serial killer on the loose but you never see a policeman round here, do you?'

'I heard the reverend was rowing with some man on the night he was attacked. Raised voices and all sorts.'

'Is that so?'

I decided it was time to move in; if the reverend's opponent was male, then Zillah was in the clear.

'Excuse me,' I said, 'but I couldn't help hearing what you said. Is it true Reverend Blackthorn was heard arguing with a man on the night he was injured?'

The man looked at me suspiciously through pebble-thick spectacles then his lined face cracked into a smile. 'Well I never. It's you, isn't it? I'm still waiting for you to take me out for that drink in The Railway Arms.'

Of course! It was the man I'd met in Burnham Market when I was in the middle of another investigation. 'Good to see you again,' I said, holding out my hand.

'I've kept your card on my mantelpiece. Rags, isn't it? A right funny name. Bet you can't remember mine.'

'Ummm ...' No good: it wouldn't come to me.

'Edward!' he said, triumphant. 'Edward North. Are you still doing your investigating?'

'I am. How about I take you for that drink?'

'Done.'

Edward had driven to Peasmarsh in his car (a nifty blue Toyota ten years younger than my old banger) after hearing about the break-in. After a short drive cross-country, along quiet B roads that skirted the walls of the Holkham estate, we met up in The Railway Arms in Burnham Market. He insisted on buying me a half of cider and a pint of bitter for himself.

Once we were settled at a table, he filled me in.

'My old pal Bert lives in sheltered housing next to St Botolph's. He don't like it much, but his old house and garden were too much for him, and he couldn't find anything he could afford in Burnham Market.' He paused to take a long, cool swallow of beer then licked his lips with pleasure.

'And he heard Reverend Blackthorn arguing with some man on the night he was injured?' I prompted.

'That's right. He thought it was odd, because the reverend's not the type to argue. In fact he's the opposite – a bit of a pushover. Gets bossed around by that secretary of his. Bert said he'd do anything for you. Mind you, he'd been acting a bit strange recently.'

'In what way?'

'Bert says he lost the thread of his sermon last Sunday more than once, and he'd never done that before.'

Another pause ensued as Edward helped himself to more swallows of beer.

'So did your friend see anything that night?'

'Well, Bert told me he was watering the pots in his back garden when he heard shouting. So he sneaks out of his garden and into the churchyard where he sees the reverend yelling at another man. He couldn't see this other man's face, but the reverend was making a heck of a noise.'

'And was this other man answering back?'

'Well that's the funny thing. The other bloke just stood

there while the reverend was shouting and shoving him around. Bert thinks he heard him say something like, "I'm sorry. I didn't *know*." Then Bert's daughter called him in for his dinner – she stops by most evenings – so Bert didn't hear the rest of it.'

'And this was around tea-time?'

'Yes. Around seven, I'd say.'

I nodded, thinking hard. Hugh Blackthorn had almost certainly cracked his head open later that evening, but could this argument be linked to his accident – if it was an accident?'And what about Zillah – the girl staying in the church? Did Bert have anything to say about her?'

'Only that she was quiet as a church mouse most of the time. Bert's always up early, and he sometimes saw her out walking. Seemed like a nice little thing.'

I sat quietly for a moment. There was something other-worldly about Zillah, but I wouldn't have described her as a 'nice little thing'.

'But one day she was making a right racket. Bert had to go round there and complain: he was being driven mad by this pounding music. Anyway, it turns out she had a friend there – a young man – no one Bert had seen before. She apologised and turned the music down, and a bit later Bert saw them both walking towards Wells.' Edward took off his spectacles and cleaned them with a handkerchief. When he slipped them back on, his eyes were sombre. 'Poor girl. I'd like to know what's happened to her.'

I asked Edward to ring me if he heard anything else then drove back to Wells under a baleful sky. When I parked the car at The Buttlands, the sun had been blotted out by blue-black clouds. A rumble of thunder was followed by a sudden downpour of hail stones. I ran through the icy onslaught towards my flat, wishing I'd thought to take a cardigan or sweatshirt with me. By the time I'd fiddled the door open – the key didn't quite fit the lock, and I had to jiggle it – I was soaked and shivering.

As I was towelling my hair dry, my phone rang.

Tracey. Again.

With a sigh, I picked up.

'It's me,' she said, her voice quieter than her usual yell. 'Zillah's mother's here and she wants to talk to you.'

Julian Lloyd was a slight woman in her forties, coiled tight as a guitar string. Her hair, cut short in the style Mia Farrow sported in *Rosemary's Baby*, was sandy-coloured and fine. I could see the resemblance between her and her daughter, but Julian had none of Zillah's radiance. She was hunched up in an oatmeal-coloured sack something like a nun's habit with a large wooden crucifix hung round her neck.

We were perched on the sofa in Tracey's lounge. The hail had stopped as abruptly as it started, and through the window I could see Tracey pegging out washing while Damon charged round the garden with a stick, bashing at plants as if he wanted to murder them. Roddy was upstairs having a nap after keeping Tracey awake most of the night.

'Reverend Blackthorn's secretary said she'd overheard him arguing with Zillah about The Sistren,' said Julian, squeezing a crumpled handkerchief between her hands, 'so the police rang and found out that I was her mother. I'm sick with worry. Suppose someone is keeping her captive?'

'That's unlikely,' I said, but without huge conviction as someone had abducted me a few months before. It hadn't been a bundle of laughs.

Julian blinked back tears. 'She wasn't ready to go into the world.'

'She was 25,' I said, trying to keep the sharpness from my voice, since to my mind Julian had virtually kept her daughter imprisoned for over a decade.

'A young 25. Impressionable.' Julian turned towards me, her face taut and pale. 'Did you know they found drug paraphernalia in her flat? Syringes, spoons. Blackened foil.'

I opened my mouth then shut it again. I hadn't seen that coming.

'And that doesn't make sense!' continued Julian, her voice hoarse with outrage. 'Zillah hated drugs. She'd seen what they could do to people in her ridiculous outreach sessions with Sister Deirdre. But the rude policewoman who telephoned gave me the impression that the police wouldn't be taking their investigation any further, "since she's an adult and may have left on her own accord." Then she said something crass about the need to select where they put their resources.'

I shook my head ruefully. That sounded all too credible.

Julian leant forward, one hand clutching her crucifix. 'That's why I want *you* to investigate what's happened to her. Find out where she's gone. Find out if she's OK.' Seeing a flicker run across my face as I mentally weighed up whether I wanted to commit myself to any more work without being paid, she added, 'I can pay you. I have money.'

I thought it over for a millisecond. 'OK. I'd be willing to do that for you.'

Closing her eyes, Julian pressed her hands into the prayer position. 'Thank you, Lord Jesus, for bringing this woman to me.'

I waited a few seconds then cleared my throat. 'My rate is £30 an hour plus expenses.'

She dug down into her canvas shoulder bag and pulled out a wadge of twenty-pound notes. 'There's three hundred pounds there. We'll see how you're getting on after you've put in ten hours.'

'Thank you.' I took the notes and slipped them into my jeans pocket.

'Can you send me an invoice and a contract?' she said, handing over a business card emblazoned with *The Sistren*, and an image of a wooden cross like the one hung round her neck, with an email address and phone number. 'I'm responsible for The Sistren's administrative work, so the emails will come directly to me.'

'Of course.'

'And regular reports?'

'Yes. And I'll do everything in my power to get to the bottom of this,' I added, because Zillah deserved it.

7

In which Rags gets on the case

I rang Zillah. She didn't answer, but I left a message asking her to call me urgently, to let me know where she was, or at least to let me know she was safe. 'And I promise anything you say will be confidential. I won't reveal where you are.'

Then I got onto the local letting agents, ringing each one with a story that I was looking for a flat to rent, saying that they'd been recommended to me by Zillah, and asking if they could let me have her address, as I needed to give her a wallet she'd left in my house by mistake. It was clear that none of them had had any contact with her.

I posted on the Facebook pages of North Norfolk groups, asking if anyone had seen her, with the same story. Unfortunately I didn't have a current photograph, but I posted the pic I'd taken of the one Tracey had, as it was still a reasonable likeness. A few replies came in swiftly from people living in and close to Peasmarsh, but all the sightings related to before the day she went missing.

I needed to talk to Evangeline Nielsen, the parish secretary, about the break-in, so rang the parish office. No one picked up. I left a message saying I'd like to speak to her about Zillah.

I spent Friday monitoring my social media posts in case any news came in of Zillah, in between hanging some curtains I'd picked up from a charity shop, and arranging my books. I fitted in a walk to Pinewoods and then along the beach to Lady Ann's Drive. A swift half at The Victoria sustained me for my walk back along the track through the woods and across the fields. A small flock of geese flew in over my head, honking, taking it in turn to pull on their rope of sky.

Seeing them, I felt a tinge of melancholy, for the arrival of the geese signals the beginning of autumn, though the days were still warm and trees still green. A little black and white dog dashed past me in pursuit of a ball, making me wish I had Napoleon to keep me company. But he and Dad were still with Susie in Cromer.

I was just settling in front of the DVD of *Working Girl* with a packet of plain crisps and a glass of wine when my phone rang. Evangeline had picked up my message and was willing to meet me in the morning.

Saturday dawned overcast. In the gauzy, grey light, the church of St Botolph's exuded a gothic gloom. The gravestones leaned like gaunt drunks. The damp breeze pushing mist up from the coast wriggled skinny fingers down my spine. Shivering, I pulled my fleece more tightly round my neck, wishing I'd worn a proper, thick sweater. I'd been fooled by the warm sun of the past couple of days, and by the cloudless skies that had welcomed me to North Norfolk when I arrived in June. This chilly damp took me back to my childhood and to the poky little house in Kings Lynn where I'd lived until I was eight.

I'd agreed to meet Evangeline at the church, where she was arranging the flowers for the Sunday services.

The heavy door yawned open with a creak when I pushed it, calling, 'Hello!'

'Come on in. I haven't got all day.'

Evangeline Nielsen was an ungainly woman with spiky dark hair. Dressed in a denim skirt, white tee-shirt and brown loafers, she was constructing a flower display of white lilies, carnations and hydrangeas. Her actions were swift, angry, as she poked the stems into the green spongy material used for flower arrangements.

'Thank you for agreeing to talk to me,' I said, walking towards her.

'I won't be long. Take a pew.'

I thought for a moment she was making a feeble but friendly witticism, but the stern look on her face told me otherwise.

Instead of sitting down I took a stroll around the church. Despite a faint smell of damp, it was a building of elegant proportions, with huge wooden roof beams arching overhead. Animal heads were carved on to the ends of the pews, their ears and noses worn down by centuries of appreciative strokes from the members of the congregation. The church was short on bling but the altar was covered in a cloth beautifully embroidered in shades of gold and green. At the other end of the nave, close to the bell tower, a display of photographs and drawings testified to a project linking the village school with one in rural Uganda. Hugh Blackthorn appeared in several of the photographs – tall, slim, with strong features and a grey ponytail falling down his back. I liked the look of him and hoped he'd recover so I could meet him. As Dad had said, he was not your conventional vicar – or, to be more accurate, he was nothing like the vicars I'd met over my journalistic career. Some had been good, kind souls, but none had sported a long ponytail and looked quite so funky in faded jeans and tee-shirt.

'Right: I can give you a few minutes now.' Evangeline's voice was harsh, tense – one of those voices with no music in it.

I hurried over, opening up my notebook. 'I know you've talked to the police,' I said, 'but Zillah's mother is desperate to find her daughter and has asked for my help. I'd appreciate it if you could tell me, informally, anything about how Zillah was getting on.'

Evangeline folded brawny arms over her chest. 'There's things you don't know about that young lady. She wasn't an innocent, for a start. You'll have heard about the drugs?'

I nodded.

'And she had a boyfriend who came to see her in the flat – a rough type from Norwich. She'll have got the drugs from him.'

'How do you know he was her boyfriend?' I asked, making a mental note to find out the identity of this 'rough type'. It sounded as if she might have met him during her outreach work with Deirdre.

'They were both lying on the bed,' said Evangeline, in a repressive tone that made it sound as if they'd been involved in an orgy.

'And you saw him more than once?'

'Two or three times. There was a complaint left on the office phone a couple of weeks back saying she and this boy had been making a nuisance of themselves playing loud music.'

I nodded. That chimed with what Edward had told me about his friend Bert complaining about Zillah and her pal making a god-awful racket. 'And he hasn't been back since?'

'Not as far as I know, but I'm only in the office three

mornings a week, so I can't be expected to see everything that goes on round here.'

I jotted down a few notes. I planned to talk to Bert, who'd probably be able to give me chapter and verse about Zillah's social life, but I had a feeling Evangeline would have heard on the grapevine if the lad had been seen again.

'But, like I say,' said Evangeline in her harsh, unforgiving voice, 'she wasn't everything she seemed. She had Hugh twisted round her little finger.'

'So, what was her state of mind in the last couple of weeks?' I said, ignoring the malice behind Evangeline's comments. 'Did she seem troubled?'

'She didn't say much to me. Kept herself to herself. But she was happy enough to latch on to Hugh. Forever rushing over and pestering him when he should have been doing church business. And he let her. You should have seen the way he looked at her – as if she were something special.'

And Zillah *was* something special – but I kept that thought to myself as I wanted to get the most I could out of Evangeline, even if a large dollop of it was malicious gossip.

'I tried to talk to him,' she continued, her voice becoming tight with suppressed tears, 'but he wouldn't listen to me. He as good as told me I was being a busybody.'

'That must have been hurtful.'

'And now he's lying in the hospital. You should see the state of him. He's got a huge bandage round his head, and he doesn't know whether he's ...' Her words dried up as she choked back tears.

'I'm sorry,' I said, seeing she was struggling. 'I can see how hard this is for you.'

'No you can't,' she said, rounding on me. 'I very much doubt you've ever had the sort of relationship I shared with Hugh.'

'And what sort of relationship was that?'

'Soul mates. We understood each other. We didn't even have to speak.'

'Were you lovers?' I asked, bluntly, irritated that she thought I'd never had a thing going with a soul mate.

Evangeline's cheeks filled with blood. 'Of course not. He was a man of the cloth.'

I didn't say the obvious – that men of the cloth have been known to have love affairs.

'Anyway,' she continued, 'I'm married.'

The surprise must have shown on my face when I glanced at her bare ring finger.

'I lost my ring a few weeks ago, if you must know,' she said, defiant. 'But my husband's buying me a new one. He's having it made specially.'

I wondered what her husband had made of his wife's obsession with the rev. Could he have become so jealous that he shoved Hugh over on to a gravestone?

'There's something else you should know,' she barked, her voice harsher than ever. 'When I went into the flat I found the cash box from the office. It was open and almost empty, but there had been at least two hundred pounds in there when I left the day before. That proves it, doesn't it? Proves that she was stealing money to pay for drugs.'

I frowned. Zillah had told me she had plenty of cash and I believed her. 'So how did she get into the office?'

'The door had been forced – but that would have been easy enough. The Yale lock was a bit loose, but we hadn't bothered because we *trusted* everyone. There had never been any trouble until that girl arrived.'

I was quiet, wondering whether Zillah would have been able to break into the office. She was young, strong fit – it wasn't inconceivable.

'Can I take a look at the flat?'

Evangeline shrugged, stuffing stalks and leaves into a carrier bag. 'If you want; the door's not locked. But you won't find anything. The police said they'd finished there so I tidied it up.'

Gritting my teeth, I thanked her and made my way round to the annex on the other side of the church. When I pushed the door open I smelled bleach. Yes, Evangeline had been at work, obliterating anything that might have given me a clue as to why Zillah had left – or been abducted. The flat, situated in what was once a side chapel, consisted of a large bedsitting room, kitchen and bathroom. It appeared to be a seventies conversion that hadn't been updated since, but it had high ceilings, beautiful windows that still had their diamond leaded lights, and austere, white walls. A small television sat on a coffee table in one corner of the room, and an old-fashioned radio was plugged in next to the cooker. The double-bed looked like it was the only piece of newish furniture – a wooden frame with a mattress of decent thickness. I looked through the chest of drawers, which contained a couple of tee shirts and a long skirt, but nothing else of interest. The wardrobe was empty except for a heavy tweed coat.

'And in case you're wondering,' came Evangeline's grating voice, 'she took her suitcase and most of her stuff with her. Seems to me she left of her own free will.'

I turned to see her standing in the doorway, her face unreadable.

'Then why was the flat trashed?'

'Perhaps her boyfriend came round and they had a fight.'

'But I heard things were broken.'

Evangeline gave a dismissive sniff. 'They were probably high on drugs. And there wasn't any serious damage – just a broken vase. The rest was just things chucked around – books on the floor – that sort of thing.'

'Where are the books now?'

Evangeline pointed. 'Back on the shelves.'

I went over and ran my eye over the titles. Most were religious texts, but there were a couple of books about nature: *Ring of Bright Water* and *Tarka the Otter.*

And at the end of the shelf, *Junky,* the William Burroughs classic hymn to heroin addiction.

Oh, crap.

8

In which Rags receives an unexpected visitor

I retreated to my car, where I fired off a text to Julian, asking her to send me the contact details of the shelter where Zillah had volunteered. I needed to talk to the 'rough type' from Norwich who'd visited her at the church, and was pretty sure she'd met him through her volunteering work.

When I got to Wells I hurried to my flat and threw the windows open. Sunshine was slowly burning through the mist rolling off the sea, and I wanted to fill my home with good vibes and chase away the poisonous miasma given off by Evangeline. I flopped on to the sofa and perhaps I fell asleep for a few minutes, because when I opened my eyes, I felt a little lighter, as if her harsh, oppressive words were slowly being diluted by the hazy blue of the sky.

I ran down the stairs, intending to buy myself a roll from the bakery, but before I got there I bumped into Toots coming out of the greengrocers with a couple of punnets of raspberries in her hands. Today she was dressed in an orange cotton dress, with a gilt chain knotted round the waist. The warm colours offset the chestnut tones of her hair. Despite her curves, her clothes fitted beautifully and I was beginning to suspect that Toots was never seen in anything but immaculate outfits.

'Rags! Do you fancy some raspberries and clotted cream?'

'But it's only half eleven,' I said, conscious of the smile spreading over my face.

'So? Raspberries can be eaten at any time of the day or night. In fact I'm sure the world would be a better place if all the sad and grumpy people were forced to eat more raspberries.'

'Raspberry therapy.'

'Precisely. Come on, then.'

She turned and started towards the quay. I jogged to catch up with her generous rump and, on impulse, threaded my arm through hers. Close to she smelt of something expensive – an intense mixture of rose, geranium and cedar. I breathed it in with a sigh of pleasure.

We walked down to the quay and turned left. A couple of hundred metres later we found our way into a yard round which five houses were clustered. She led me towards the one furthest away, whitewashed and surrounded by pots spilling scarlet, pink and white geraniums. As she washed the raspberries and shook them dry, she asked me what I'd been up to. I told her that I was looking into Zillah's disappearance.

'I went to talk to Evangeline this morning, at the church,' I began, 'and she had some interesting things to say.'

Toots gave me a sharp look. 'Don't be too hard on her. I've known her for years. She was very kind to me when I lost my husband. Used to come round with fresh flowers – that sort of thing. She's not had the easiest time of it.'

Once we were settled at the kitchen table with bowls of ripe raspberries topped with generous dollops of thick cream, I asked her to elaborate.

'She was doing OK until she got married. She'd been single for ever, with a permanent but harmless crush on Hugh, until Terry swept her off her feet a couple of years ago.' We spooned fragrant raspberries into our mouths and enjoyed them silently for a few seconds before she spoke again. 'And he's a charmer – rough round the edges but handsome in a weather-beaten sort of way. Used to work on the crab boats until he had an accident a few years back. Anyway, it turned out he'd developed a shopping habit while he was laid low after his accident – he was forever buying gadgets he didn't need and ended up with a huge credit card debt.

Evangeline knew nothing about it until the debt collectors came calling. But she's stood by him; she cut up all his cards and keeps an eagle eye on their joint finances. He had a job in one of the pubs, but was sacked when they suspected he had his fingers in the till, though they couldn't prove anything. That was about a year ago and he's not had regular work since. He does bits and pieces of building work and gardening – he's good at it, too – but we all know not to leave cash or valuables lying around.'

'But people still give him work?'

Toots shrugged, releasing a gust of her delicious scent. 'This is a small community, and at heart he's a good man. He was born here, and we don't turn on our own.'

'And what about you? Were you born here?'

That provoked another gust of laughter. 'No way, Jose. I was born in Hertfordshire and spent most of my working life in London.'

'Doing what?'

More luscious raspberries found their way into her mouth. 'Guess.'

I considered her for a moment. 'Something theatrical?'

'After a fashion.'

'Actress? Theatrical agent? Singer? Trapeze artist?'

'Barrister. For a while, at least. I stuck it for about a decade then packed it in to do something I loved. I had a small vintage clothes shop around the back of The Angel. Sold up a few years back. Made a packet on my grotty little Islington flat and moved up here. Me and my husband decided to relocate to Wells when he took early retirement from teaching. He was head of a primary school: the children adored him, but he was exhausted with all the admin.' A flicker of pain ran across her face. 'He died three years ago, unexpectedly.'

'I'm so sorry.'

She threw me a brief, sad smile. 'We'd had a bloody good innings. And what about you?'

'Single at the moment.'

She raised her eyebrows, inviting me to say more.

'But I lived with my partner, for a long while.' Then, after a pause, 'until he left me for his pregnant secretary.'

'Ouch.'

I finished up my raspberries, avoiding her gaze because a lump had appeared in my throat. Oh, come on, Rags, I told myself. That was five years and a couple of love affairs ago. Get over it.

'Coffee?'

'That would be lovely. Thank you.'

As she filled the espresso pot we chatted about lighter subjects – my flat, the new literature festival that had succeeded Poetry-Next-the-Sea, the best song by the late, lamented Prince (*1999* for her, *Purple Rain* for me). Then, when we were settled, I returned to the subject of Zillah.

'Did you meet her?'

Toots shook her head. 'But I saw her once, walking along the bank towards Pinewoods. A friend pointed her out to me - we were driving up to the car park to take her dog for a walk. I was interested because Evangeline had been grumbling to me about her staying at St Botolph's.' She paused as she got out a couple of green glazed mugs.

'And?' I prompted.

'And she hinted that there was something going on between the girl and Hugh.'

'Did you believe that?'

She thought for a moment. 'Not to begin with; Hugh was such a nice, ethical man that I couldn't imagine him getting embroiled with a much younger woman. But I tried to talk to him one night in The Eddie and he was all over the place – couldn't hold a proper conversation.' She shrugged. 'The human heart is a funny thing. It can make you do crazy things.'

'And the drugs? I expect you've heard drugs gubbins were found in the flat.'

'Yes. Everyone in Wells was talking about it. Sorry. I can't help you with that.' She frowned then her face cleared 'But I think she and Alfie knew each other. You remember him, don't you? He's hoping to be cast as Bertie Wooster in *Jeeves Pulls it Off*. I saw him and Zillah walking along the coast path close to the East Quay one day, deep in conversation.'

'Thanks. Have you got his number?'

'Hang on. I'll find it for you.' She pulled open a drawer of a pine bureau and got out a typed list of names and contact details for the Peasmarsh Players. 'Here you are. He runs holiday lets – Blue Sky Cottages – on his parents' estate.'

I thanked her, and took my leave. Not only had she provided me with raspberries, she'd also given me a lead to pursue.

As I was near The Maltings, I dropped in there to pick up a leaflet about Blue Sky Cottages from the Tourist Information display. The flyer informed that the cottages, a couple of miles from Wells, were beautifully appointed and that everyone arrived to a welcome basket 'containing fruit, flowers, coffee, milk and local home-made biscuits.'

For a few minutes I browsed the other flyers and posters, finding that I could go seal watching from Morston, or catch the little train that ran from Wells to Walsingham. I could watch an Alan Ayckbourn play at West Acre, or drop into one of the productions in rep at Sheringham Little Theatre. I smiled to myself. Though I'd left London out of desperation, I'd landed on my feet. I had my own flat in a funky seaside town. I had work and I was making new friends.

When I was back on the street I rang Blue Sky Cottages hoping to speak to Alfie; no one answered so I left a message.

Then, while I was walking back to my flat, my phone rang. Dad.

'Hi, Dad. Are you back in Fakenham?'

'Rags! We need to have a chat.' His voice broke up then returned, crackly. 'I'm out for a walk with Napoleon, and haven't got much of a signal, but I promise I'll ...'

And then the connection was cut.

I frowned. What was all that about? I thought for a moment but couldn't come up with an answer. Never mind: I was sure he'd ring again when he had a proper signal.

Meanwhile I had work to do. I knew I needed to update Julian with what I'd learned from Evangeline, but first I'd have something to eat; the raspberries had been delicious but my stomach was rumbling. As I got closer to my flat I debated how much I should tell her. So far I had no good news to deliver. The visitor from Norwich sounded deeply dodgy, and I knew she wouldn't want to hear about the empty cash box and drug paraphernalia found in Zillah's flat. Could she have been dabbling in drugs? Sometimes people kept on a short leash for a long time do reckless things when they're finally released.

Yet it still felt all wrong.

Oh sod it. I'd have a cheese roll then decide what to do next.

As I approached my flat I saw that a slender woman with drifts of pale-gold hair was perched on a suitcase outside my front door.

Curious, I quickened my pace. The woman didn't see me coming: she was rooting around in a hippyish shoulder bag, her face obscured by the strands of her hair dancing in the breeze running up from the coast.

Then she lifted her head and looked straight at me. I faltered, stopped in my tracks. It couldn't be. Surely not.

But it was. The woman called, 'Ragnell! Angel!' and ran towards me, arms outstretched. In seconds she'd thrown her arms round me, enveloping me in a musky cloud of patchouli.

Gwendolyn. My mother.

9

In which we learn a little about Gwendolyn

'What the hell are you doing here?' I croaked, once I'd got my breath back. 'You're supposed to be in Florida.'

'Graham gave me your address. Oh, let me look at you.'

Ah. That explained Dad's anxious phone call.

'My little girl. I've been longing to see you.'

I wanted to tell her to cut the crap. She'd never been much of a mother to me. When I was a kid she'd spent most of her time lying on the sofa painting her nails purple and reading palmistry magazines. Then, after she dumped Dad for Nigel and dragged me off to Devon, she'd reserved most of her maternal affection for Tarquin, my half-brother, who came along when I was twelve. She'd been living in a retirement village in Florida for the past decade and didn't even remember to send me a birthday card most years: I was lucky if I received an email a day late, full of gushing apologies.

'Why are you here?'

'Do I have to have a reason to visit my lovely daughter?'

She batted false eyelashes at me and I had to admit she looked pretty stunning for a woman in her early sixties. Slim as willow, her face barely lined (due to the wonders of Botox, I was sure, since she'd had more crows' feet the last time I saw her), she looked chic in a pair of skinny white jeans and a simple pink shirt. To my dismay I felt a pang of envy; I was no bag of spanners, but Gwendolyn was a beauty in another league.

'Well yes, you do,' I said, hardening my heart. 'I haven't heard from you in ages and the last time we spoke you said you were never coming back to Britain because it was such a dump.'

She stiffened. 'Why are you being so cruel?'

'Just tell me why you're here.'

Her lower lip trembled. 'I've ... I've left Nigel.'

That shut me up for a few seconds. 'I suppose you'd better come in then,' I said.

Light on her feet, she bounded ahead of me as I dragged her monster case up the stairs. Once we were in the flat she demanded a cup of tea. 'Camomile or nettle, please. I need to cleanse myself after the energy pollution of my journey.'

I had a few dusty camomile tea bags in the kitchen cupboard so, muttering under my breath, I made her a cup, and got myself a glass of water. As she blew on her tea and I sipped at my water, I felt my heartbeat slowing down. So Gwendolyn was here. I'd just have to deal with it.

'OK. Tell me what's happened. Why have you left him? I thought you were perfectly aligned, energetically speaking. At least that's what you told me six months ago.'

'Why do you think?' She blinked back tears from luminous green eyes. 'He's having an affair.'

'What?'

'With a Las Vegas pole dancer.'

I opened my mouth then shut it again. Nigel? Pole dancer? It just didn't compute.

Seeing my scepticism, Gwendolyn pulled a brand new iPhone out of her bag and scrolled through to a photograph of Nigel snogging a woman dressed only in scarlet sequinned underwear and a feathered head dress.

'I can't stand infidelity. Once I discovered the truth, I had to leave.'

Talk about kettles and pots. Gwendolyn had torn Dad's heart into tatters when she ran off with Nigel. 'Karma, more like,' I muttered.

'What was that?' she snapped, her face hardening into the mask I remembered from my childhood whenever she was crossed.

'Nothing,' I muttered, because I didn't want to get into an argument with her in the first five minutes of our reunion.

'So I caught the first plane to England. I was sure your father would help me in my hour of need, but I got cut off in the middle of our conversation.' She arranged her face into a wistful smile. 'Then I had a brainwave. I decided to spend some special time with you!' She leant forward, clasping her hands together. 'It'll give us a chance to *bond*.'

'I don't have a spare room,' I said, seeing where this was going.

'It won't be for long. I'm sure Nigel will transfer some money into my account any day now.' She ran her fingers through ash-blonde extensions that must have cost a few hundred dollars. 'Until he does I'm rather low on funds. I couldn't believe how much it cost to take a taxi from the airport.'

The blood rushed to my head. 'Why didn't you catch the train and the bus, like the rest of us?'

'So you see I'm throwing myself on your mercy.' She took a sip of tea and batted her eyelashes at me again. 'It's either that or I'll have to persuade your father to take me in.'

The nerve of the woman! She'd always been able to twist Dad round her little finger despite their bitter break-up. I pondered for a few seconds then came to the only possible conclusion. I couldn't put Dad through that. His budding relationship with Susie would be ruined by him having to attend to Gwendolyn.

'You can stay here until the money from Nigel comes through. Then I'll help you find somewhere more suitable.'

She jumped up from the sofa and gave me a patchouli scented hug. 'Thank you so much, darling. I knew you'd say yes. And I promise I'll be quiet as a mouse – you'll hardly know I'm here.'

I gave her the bedroom, grumbling under my breath as I changed the sheets and pillowcases. She was a monumental pain in the arse, but she was my mother, a woman of 63 who needed a decent bed. I could sleep on anything, and would be fine on the sofa bed in the lounge. Whatever had happened with the pole dancer, Nigel was besotted with Gwendolyn and would soon come running back with his tail between his legs.

Wouldn't he?

I dragged her case upstairs and left her to settle in. Ten minutes later, feeling I must offer her something to eat, I went upstairs and tapped on the bedroom door. Getting no reply I pushed it open, thinking she might have fallen asleep after her long flight. But she was sitting cross-legged on the rug, eyes closed.

Hearing the door, she opened one eye and gave

me a tetchy look. 'I don't like to be disturbed while I'm meditating.'

'I just wondered whether you wanted some lunch.'

'Not until I've spoken to my spirit guides,' she said, closing her eyes again.

'I've got to go out for a couple of hours,' I said, because I needed to talk to Dad, and preferably meet up with him, as soon as possible. 'Make yourself at home. Help yourself to whatever you want – there's salad, cheese and bread.'

'And coffee?' squawked Gwendolyn, reminding me that she'd been way ahead of her time with her insatiable appetite for caffeine.

'There's plenty in the fridge and a pot on the stove or filter papers in the cupboard, if you prefer it made that way.'

'Ah, so you did learn something from me,' she said, with a smug smile before closing her eyes again.

'And there's a spare key on the hook by the door if you want to go out and explore Wells,' I said as I left the room, closing the bedroom door behind me.

As soon as I was outdoors I rang Dad, praying he'd be back home, because we had to devise a joint strategy to deal with Gwendolyn. What's more, I needed to email a report to Julian – something I couldn't do from the flat, as BT Openworld still hadn't deigned to give me an appointment to set up my broadband service. I could have gone to a cafe, or fiddled around with my phone but it would be easier to work at Dad's house.

Thankfully he picked up.

'I'm sorry,' he started, the happy, confident Dad of the past few weeks obliterated by one phone call from Gwendolyn. 'I didn't mean to give her your address, not until I'd talked to you, but she got it out of me.'

'Don't worry, Dad. I know what she's like.'

'She started on about needing somewhere to stay, and

I just panicked. I cut her off. I shouldn't have done that, should I?'

'I've told her she can stay with me.'

'Oh, Rags, you didn't have to do that,' he said, the relief flooding his voice.

'Yes, I did. I'll take care of it – of her,' I said, because I was not going to let Gwendolyn bugger up his life again. 'But we need to talk. Can I come over?'

'Of course. I'll make us a spot of lunch. It'll just be Heinz tomato soup, bread and cheese.'

'Thanks, Dad. That would be fantastic. I'm starving.'

10

In which Rags and Dad console each other

As I walked along the shared path that runs between the back yards and the gardens of The Terrace I heard Napoleon start to bark and quickened my pace. As I did, the gate to Dad's back yard opened, and Napoleon appeared – a blur of black and white dashing towards me. I bent down and scooped him up into my arms, submitting to a volley of happy kisses. I gave him a hug then put him down. He treated himself to a full body shake then trotted beside me to Dad's house. Napoleon's like that: he's delighted to see you, but once you've exchanged greetings, he settles down and offers a calmer companionship. Dad appeared, with an apron showing a map of North Norfolk tied round his waist.

'Perfect timing. I'm just serving up.'

I followed him into the sunny kitchen, which was just large enough to hold a small table and two chairs, and we tucked into lunch. As I buttered a slice of wholemeal bread, which Dad informed me was from a new market stall, I felt the knots in my shoulders start to come loose. All was well with the world if I had Dad, Napoleon, and a bowl of Heinz tomato soup.

We made small talk before plunging into the knotty problem of how to deal with Gwendolyn. He told me about the walk he'd taken with Napoleon that morning. 'Beyond the lake on the Holkham Estate. I'd not been there before. Napoleon liked it, didn't you, boy?' Napoleon gave a small bark of assent.

I described a couple of plates I'd seen in the charity shop. 'I don't really need them, but they're a gorgeous bird of paradise design.'

'You love that sort of thing, don't you?' said Dad. 'And you can afford them.'

Yes, with the help of the money I'd earned that summer, I'd started repaying the considerable debts I'd run up in London and had been feeling pretty contented until my troublesome mother turned up on the doorstep. I gave a little groan and a moment later a cold, wet nose pushed at my leg; Napoleon had picked up on my gloomy thoughts and was doing his usual trick of offering wordless consolation. Grateful, I stroked his head and silky ears.

'You're right,' I said to Dad. 'I'll get those plates the next time I'm in the shop.'

Dad cleared the table, switched on the kettle and sat down again. 'So, what are we going to do about your mother?'

Napoleon gave a long sigh and flopped on to the floor.

'You're not going to do anything. I'll email Nigel and ask him, as tactfully as possible, to stop buggering around and come and collect her, or, at the very least, send her some funds.'

'And do you think he will?'

'It's worth a try. And I'll contact Tarquin, too. He sees

a lot more of Gwendolyn and might have a better idea of how things stand.' I pulled out my phone. 'In fact I'll call him now.'

Tarquin picked up after the first ring. 'Hi there, big sis! To what do I owe the pleasure?'

A smile broke over my face. My little step-brother is irrepressibly camp and good tempered. 'It's about Gwendolyn.'

'Oh lord!' I heard the palm of his hand hit his forehead. 'What's she done now?'

'Well ...' I let a dramatic pause open up. 'She's turned up on my doorstep. Says she's left Nigel.'

'What?'

'You hadn't heard?'

'Not a dicky-bird.'

I sighed. Trust Gwendolyn to land herself on me and Dad rather than Tarquin.

'But why?'

'She says he's been unfaithful.'

Tarquin's exclamation of disbelief came over loud and clear from New York.

'With a Las Vegas pole dancer.'

'Oh p-lease,' he drawled, using one of the expressions we shared when talking about our parents. 'He wouldn't know a pole dancer if one jumped out from behind a tree and bit him on the bum.'

'She's shown me a picture.'

A thoughtful silence followed.

'How have they been getting on lately?' I asked.

'Same as usual as far as I can see. She spends a fortune on courses and gurus and he grumbles and plays golf.'

I sighed, disappointed that Tarquin wasn't able to shed any light on the situation.

'Look,' he said, 'I'll ask around a bit. I'm in contact with a gay couple who are their chums in the seniors' village. They'll let me have the latest goss.'

I thanked him, and asked how things were going – he's an uber-trendy milliner in Manhattan. 'Mustn't grumble. My regulars keep me busy, and there are some big fundraisers coming up this autumn that will keep me in bran flakes and champagne.'

'And how's Godfrey?' I asked, referring to his long term boyfriend – a beautiful young Puerto Rican who'd been strutting his stuff as a model when Tarquin met him.

'Divine as ever. In fact we might even tie the knot next year.'

'Congratulations!'

'Thank you. And don't worry about the mum thing. You know what she's like: it'll probably turn out to be a storm in a teacup.'

I felt reassured by my conversation with Tarquin. He'd spent far more time with them than I had – I'd left home when he was six – and if he wasn't too worried, than I shouldn't be, either.

Dad, too, looked relieved. 'So he'll get back to you when he knows how things stand?'

'Yes. But I'll email Nigel, and ask him, as tactfully as possible, to set her up with funds so she can sort out somewhere to stay. Could I email him from here? I've still got no broadband.'

'Of course.'

'And I've got a report to write.' I tapped my shoulder bag. 'I've got my laptop with me.'

'What's the report about?'

'I've taken on a new case,' I said then swiftly outlined Zillah's story. When I'd finished Dad held up his finger, just as he had when I was seven and wanting to run out to play in the dark.

'Promise me you'll never get mixed up in anything to do with drugs.'

'I promise,' I said, because drugs held no appeal. Oh, I'd dabbled in my time, but had soon realised they didn't do it for me.

'Because I couldn't stand it if I ...' He cleared his throat. ' ... if I lost you.'

'I promise,' I repeated. 'I know the dangers.'

He let out a breath of relief. 'That's all right then. I'm going to change some library books so I'll leave you in peace.' He clipped a lead on Napoleon and left by the back door.

It didn't take me long to write up the notes of my investigation into Zillah's disappearance, and they didn't make for cheerful reading. I tried to put a positive spin on it, saying that it was early days blah, blah, but I had a sinking feeling as I pressed Send. What mother wants to read that drug-taking gubbins and an empty cashbox were found in her daughter's flat?

I then turned to composing an email to Nigel, and that wasn't a piece of cake, either.

Hi there, Nigel,
You'll be glad to know that Gwendolyn is safe and well. She's staying with me for the time being. I was sorry to hear of the difficulties between the two of you, and hope you will soon be reconciled. She urgently needs money and I'm afraid I'm not in a position to lend her any. She's said she's waiting for you to transfer funds into her account. Could you please do that as soon as possible? Thanks. It would be good to talk. Please ring me on 07878 5444365 when you can.
With love and best wishes,
Rags

That'll do, I told myself. It's short and to the point.

Within seconds a reply pinged back: Auto-Reply. *I'm on vacation for the foreseeable future. I will pick up emails once a week. I can't be reached by telephone.*

Damn.

When Dad returned he found me looking dejected. I showed him Nigel's Auto-Reply message. 'Where the hell has he gone?' I asked. 'He never goes away without her.'

Dad groaned. 'Nothing that involves Gwendolyn is ever simple.'

My phone pinged: Julian, acknowledging my report, and sending me the number of A Place to Call Home, the charity for the homeless with whom Zillah had volunteered.

I gave them a call, and briefly explained the situation with Zillah, saying that I was hoping to talk to a friend I thought she'd made while volunteering with Deidre. The manager, whose name was Marianne, suggested that I visit the hostel that evening. 'I think I know the friend you're talking about: Laurie. He's a lovely young man. He doesn't often stay here – we only have eight beds – but he might drop in tonight. We cook an evening meal for anyone who needs it and he often shows up.'

I thanked her, and we agreed to meet at around half five, so we could have a chat first.

11

*In which Rags finds out about
Zillah's life in Norwich*

I returned to Wells, feeling more composed and intending
to talk to Gwendolyn about the situation with Nigel.

But she was out. Relieved at postponing our conversation,
I left her a note and set off for Norwich in my car. After
finding a parking place in one of Norwich's multi-storey
car parks I found A Place to Call Home with the help of
Google maps. It was located in a narrow cul-de-sac close
to the river – a cool street overshadowed by tall buildings.
Two large terracotta pots spilled red geraniums beside the
entrance to the shelter.

When I knocked, the door was swiftly opened, and a
face framed in thick, sandy dreadlocks beamed at me.

'Rags, is it?'

'Yes. Thanks for agreeing to see me.'

She extended her hand. 'My pleasure. I'm Marianne.
Come on in. I haven't see Laurie for a few days, but I'm
hoping he'll eat here this evening.' Her genial face became

serious. 'He should be able to tell you about Zillah: I've realised he's very fond of her.'

'I appreciate you taking the time to see me.'

'No probs. Let's talk in my office.' She unlocked the door to a small, neat room perfumed with something delicious. 'Incense,' she said, noting my reaction. 'I go to India every winter for a few weeks to recharge my batteries and always bring some home. Please, take a seat.'

'I went to Kerala when I was younger,' I said, remembering drifting up and down the backwaters in a small boat with Matt, my then partner, while a guide pointed out the brilliantly coloured birds swooping in and out of the palm trees. At the time I'd been a trainee journalist in rural Yorkshire, while he was starting out in radio production. A small part of me ached for those simpler times, powered by certainty and hope.

'Do you fancy a coffee?' asked Marianne. 'I'm going to have one.'

'That would be lovely,' I said, bringing myself firmly back to the present, and got out my notebook as she spooned fresh coffee into a cafetiere. Her office was painted yellow and blue – strong primary colours – with a set of shelves on which books were arranged in sections, a large whiteboard, and a notice board on which rotas and statutory notices were pinned. Beside her desk she'd stuck a few posters of musicians, none of which I recognised except Christine and the Queens.

'So: how can I help you?' she asked, once the water had been poured over the coffee grains.

'I'm looking for Zillah on behalf of her mother. She was living for a while at St Botolph's church in Peasmarsh, but she hasn't been seen since someone broke into her flat and the police won't take it any further. When did you last see her?'

Marianne thought for a moment. 'Several weeks ago, I think. I ran into her with her suitcase. She told me she was on the way to the bus station and didn't have time to chat.'

I nodded. 'She was probably on her way to Peasmarsh.'

'But now she's gone missing?'

'Yes, and I'm trying to find out where she's gone, and whether she's safe.' I paused. 'Do you think she was someone who might be attracted to drug use?'

Marianne shook her head firmly. 'I never saw any evidence of that.'

At the mention of Zillah's disappearance her face had lost its positive shine, and I realised she was older than I'd first thought – in her late thirties, perhaps.

'Can you tell me what you made of her?'

'I only met her three times. The first time was just before Christmas last year. She came with Sister Deirdre to help with the evening meal; the local supermarkets had donated loads of festive food close to its sell-by date. I remember she was very shy – hardly said a word. She kept herself to herself and stayed in the kitchen for most of the evening, prepping veg, making tea and washing up.'

'Did you talk to her?'

'Only a few words. I welcomed her and thanked her for coming along. She blushed and mumbled that it was nothing: she was happy to be doing God's work.'

'And the next time?'

'She was a different person. I'd been away in India so it was the end of March before I next ran into her. This time I was on the street beat. It was freezing cold, so we were going round with blankets in case anyone needed them. Deidre and Zillah had gone on ahead with another member of staff, while I dealt with a problem here. When I came across them they were sharing a flask of tea and some sandwiches with Laurie and a couple of his mates on the flight of steps close to the town hall. Zillah was laughing at some joke Laurie had cracked. The first time I saw her she'd had her hair hidden under a scarf, but now it was loose. She looked absolutely beautiful – like something out of a Burne-Jones painting.'

'Did you talk to her?'

'Yes. I can't remember exactly what we said, but she was far more animated and forthcoming. She asked me about my trip to India, and Laurie said he'd always wanted to go. She gave him the sweetest, most open smile and I hoped she wasn't going to get her heart broken. He's a lovely young man, but like many of our clients, his life is chaotic.'

'Do you think they were in a relationship?'

'No. I didn't get that impression. For a start, she was always accompanied by Deirdre, who was very protective, though I suppose she could have hooked up with Laurie when Deirdre wasn't around.'

'And the third time?'

'That was when I saw her with her suitcase heading for the bus station. I ran to catch up with her, but she didn't want to talk. She said she was going away for a few weeks, and had to hurry as she had a bus to catch.' She sighed. 'I hoped she might come back, perhaps do an internship or train as a social worker.'

'And what do you know about The Sistren?'

'I'd heard about them – everyone in Norwich knows they're a closed community of Christian women – but they only started doing outreach work when Sister Deirdre joined them. She'd been through some difficult times herself, and wanted to contribute something to society. Mind you, I had the feeling that the head of The Sistren wasn't too keen on her ideas.'

No kidding, I thought.

'Deidre took a shine to Zillah: she could see she needed

to spread her wings.' Marianne's face clouded over. 'Deirdre came to see me after Zillah left The Sistren. Apparently she'd been given her marching orders by the head of the community. I asked her where she'd go, and she shrugged her shoulders and said she was going back to London. That worried me.' She leaned forward, hands clasped. 'I wouldn't last a week in a community like The Sistren, but it gives some people the structure and support they need. For all her streetwise experience, Deirdre was vulnerable.' She shook her head, lips pressed together. 'But I expected Zillah to thrive once she got out into the world.'

I thanked her. We talked about other things for a while. She volunteered that she was an alcoholic who'd got sober a decade ago, after a few years falling in and out of sobriety, then directed me to Phil, a Scottish man with a worn, kind face who'd accompanied Zillah when she volunteered with people living on the streets. He confirmed what she'd said about Zillah but could add nothing new. 'She was a lassie with a good heart. I could see she was taken with Laurie, but to me it looked like a schoolgirl crush.' Like Marianne, he hadn't seen any signs that Zillah might be drawn to drugs, adding, 'though you never can tell who'll be tempted.'

It was now just after six, and people were starting to drift into the dining room, a large room simply furnished with tables and chairs, but painted, like Marianne's office, in bright colours, this time green and orange. A mixture of volunteers and residents were serving vegetable stew and baked potatoes with grated cheese.

I waited for Laurie, but after an hour he hadn't turned up. Disappointed, I returned to Marianne's office. Through the half-open door I could see her feeding figures into her laptop from a pile of paperwork. When I tapped she looked up and beckoned me in. Told there was no sign of Laurie, she came through to the dining room, where the last diners were finishing their meal. Going over to one youngish man who looked as if he'd be more at home in a bank were it not for his tatty clothes, she asked him a few questions then returned to me shaking her head.

'He says he hasn't seen Laurie for a while.'

A shiver ran from my scalp to my toes.

'Tell you what, I'll give you a ring when I next see him.' She put on what I was beginning to recognise as her positive face. 'I'm sure he's OK.'

As I returned to my car, uncomfortable questions started to form in my head.

What had happened to Laurie?

And did he have anything to do with Zillah's disappearance?

12

In which Rags talks to Alfie Adams

By the time I got back to Wells, Alfie Adams had left a message on my phone, saying he could meet me at Blue Sky Cottages at nine-thirty the following morning. There was no sign of Gwendolyn, so I went to bed, assuming she was asleep upstairs.

The next thing I knew the smell of fresh coffee was drifting up my nose. I prised my eyes open to see Gwendolyn in my tiny kitchen making a pot of espresso coffee on the stove. As soon as it approached boiling point she turned off the heat – she does have some talents – and set about finding cups and saucers.

'Good morning,' she cried. 'I thought you might like a coffee.'

'Thank you,' I croaked, vocal cords still foggy with sleep.

'Here.' Moments later a small cup of coffee smelling deliciously strong appeared on the side table next to my head. 'And here's some sugar.'

Gwendolyn perched on the small armchair opposite,

regarding me with a beatific smile I found a tad disturbing. She was dressed in a floaty skirt, pale cream with an eau de nil pattern, and a plain white tee-shirt that looked decidedly expensive.

'I hope I didn't wake you last night.'

She raised her eyebrows. 'Actually, I was out myself until midnight.' Then, with a dreamy smile, 'watching the moon on the water.'

'I didn't hear you come in.'

'I promised to be no trouble.'

'Thank you for being so considerate,' I said, determined to be kind, welcoming. I added a spoon of soft brown sugar to my coffee and took a sip: pure caffeine nectar.

'I spent the evening with some like-minded souls. It was divine.' She took a deep breath. 'And through the medium of a unique spiritual leader, I was able to progress to another plane of being.'

'Sounds fascinating,' I said, trying to keep my voice neutral. 'Who was this spiritual leader?'

'Don't be nosy!'

'I'm not being nosy. Just interested.'

She ran her fingers through her blonde locks. 'I thought you were dismissive of spiritual matters.'

I could feel my hackles rising. Conversations with Gwendolyn often went like this. They started innocuously, then strayed into frustrating backwaters where she wouldn't say what she meant, or made sly digs. I finished my coffee in silence.

'Well?' she said. 'Are you?'

'Am I what?'

'Dismissive of spiritual matters. Only I've always picked up that you're like your father: an earthbound cynic.'

I was disconcerted to feel tears pricking at my eyes. For as long as I could remember Gwendolyn had taunted me about being unspiritual. I couldn't face it at this time in the morning. Besides, I had an investigation to pursue.

I struggled to my feet. 'I'm sorry, but I've got to get going. I've got work to do.'

'Now? It's only quarter past eight.'

'I've got an early appointment,' I said, thinking I could pick up some breakfast along the coast before I met up with Alfie. If I stayed here with Gwendolyn I'd just get more and more wound up. 'I'll have a quick shower and then be off.'

With that, I dashed upstairs and into the bathroom. After a lightning shower I pulled on a pair of skinny black jeans and a red sweater, since clouds were massing in the sky and the temperature was several degrees cooler than the last few days. Hearing chanting coming from the bedroom, I hurried out of the flat and into a grey and gloomy Staithe Street.

I was grumbling under my breath as I headed towards my car. Yes, I do have an interest in spirituality, and I'm sure there are forces at work that we don't understand. I've felt the presence of people who have died, and I'm pretty damn sure I've experienced a telepathic connection with people close to me at crucial times in my life. But I'm wary of gurus and the like. I know they're helpful for some people, but they can also be dangerous, harmful, whether they're espousing New Age beliefs, or lodged within the well established world religions, most of whom seem hell bent on shaming and blaming women.

With a conscious effort, I pushed these weighty thoughts from my mind and headed east along the coast road through a haze of drizzle. As I had time to kill, I decided to head to Blakeney for a bite to eat. I wanted to be sure I wouldn't run into someone I knew and needed some head space to process what was happening with Gwendolyn.

My breakfast in Blakeney was disappointing. The coffee was watery and the croissant dry. But the view was to die for, even though it was partly shrouded in mist – the path on the raised bank winding past the moored and abandoned boats towards the rhythmic song of the waves. I lingered over my coffee, reading through my notes and making an effort to focus on the job in hand. Julian wanted answers, and I was determined to get them for her and Zillah.

At half past nine I paid for my breakfast and headed for a spot of bird watching at the pond beside the car park where ducks, coots, swans, geese and other waterfowl were preening, feeding and doing other birdy things. I took pleasure in watching them, remembering the heavenly walk I'd taken earlier in the summer with Dad and Napoleon at the Cley nature reserve. Then I returned to my car and gave Alfie a ring. He confirmed that he was in his office, and gave me instructions on how to get there – helpful, as the directions provided by my phone are hit and miss once you get off the main roads.

Just before 10.00 I tapped on Blue Sky's office door. It was opened immediately, with a theatrical flourish. Alfie, still debonair but wearing jeans and a striped shirt, led me into a spacious office in what must once have been a stable, with huge, classy photographs of North Norfolk displayed on the walls: Blakeney, Cley Marshes, Holkham, Brancaster, Wells, Salthouse church. I noticed that Fakenham, Dad's no-nonsense market town, didn't feature among them.

'Beautiful photographs. Did you take them?'

He grinned. 'No. They were taken by a friend of mine. We were at school together. Not bad, are they?'

'They're fabulous.'

Alfie invited me to sit down and asked whether I wanted coffee. I accepted, since the watery brew at the Blakeney cafe had left me craving another decent hit of caffeine. He had a machine that took coffee pods – machines I privately thought were a waste of time and ecologically suspect. But the espresso he placed in front of me was strong and flavoursome. I thanked him and asked him whether he'd heard about the part of Bertie Wooster in *Jeeves Pulls it Off*.

'Not yet, but I haven't heard that anyone else has been cast as Bertie, so fingers crossed.'

'I hope you get it. You'd be perfect.'

He beamed, nodding his thanks, then asked, 'So what did you want to talk to me about?'

'Zillah, the young woman who was staying at St Botolph's has disappeared under troubling circumstances, and I wondered if you could shed any light on what might have happened. I gather you know her.'

'Not really. I only met her once, and that was about three weeks ago, at the start of the coastal path close to the East Quay at Wells. I like to take a stroll there when I've finished shopping or banking in Wells to clear my head before coming back to the office. We walked together for a while, and she asked me how far the path ran. I explained that it went all the way to Cromer.'

'And how did she seem?'

He frowned. 'A bit lost,' he said, finally. 'She told me it was weird living independently for the first time.'

'So she told you about her years with The Sistren.'

'Yes. She said she hadn't been allowed to do normal teenage things like going out with mates.'

I nodded. 'And she seemed a bit lost?' I prompted.

He hesitated. 'She said she was having trouble sleeping and asked me whether I could get her anything that would help. I told her to go to her GP, but she said she didn't have one at the moment and then ...' He paused, avoiding my gaze.

'And then what?'

'This is confidential, isn't it?'

'Absolutely.'

He sighed. 'She asked me whether I could score some drugs for her.'

'What did she want?'

He paused then forged on. 'Just dope, but I was a bit taken aback. She didn't seem the type.'

'And did you help her out?'

A blush crept up his thin cheeks. 'Of course not. She was a vulnerable girl, and I didn't want to encourage her to get involved in any sort of drug taking. Anyway, we'd only just met.'

'And she accepted that?'

'Seemed to.' He opened his mouth as if to say something more then shut it again.

'What? What else did she say?'

'She said someone had told her you could buy heroin in Kings Lynn. I told her that was a bad, bad idea, but she just laughed. "I'll be fine. Don't worry about me." That was what she said.'

A nasty, cold feeling shifted around the bottom of my stomach.

'Did she tell you she'd been volunteering at a Norwich shelter?'

He frowned, thinking back. 'Yes. And she mentioned a friend she'd met there. She said he'd visited her once or twice. I got the impression she was keen on him.'

'Do you remember his name?'

'Something beginning with L – Larry ... something like that.'

My spirits sank: this had to be the same person.

'And soon after that I had to split,' Alfie continued. 'New guests were arriving and I had to rush back here. They have a hissy fit if you're not at their beck and call.'

Right on cue, as I jotted down a few notes, someone rapped on the door. With a muttered apology Alfie opened it, putting on his professional smile as he did so. A woman in one of those shapeless, linen dresses popular with well-heeled women stood there with a fierce scowl on her face, holding up an earthenware mug and complaining that it was cracked. 'And one of the plant pots is chipped. For the money we're paying, we expect better.'

He apologised profusely, adding, 'I'll be with you in two ticks.' When he'd shut the door on her he pulled a face, muttering, 'You see what I have to put up with?'

'And you haven't seen Zillah since?' I said, gathering up my things ready to leave.

'No. We swapped numbers, but that's all.'

'You've been so helpful. Thanks for your time.'

'My pleasure. I hope she turns up safe.'

As he was ushering me out, his phone rang and I was able to read the caller's name: Hengist. Alfie's face lit up. He shut the door firmly behind me but I couldn't resist glancing through the window, expecting to see his face wreathed in smiles. Instead Alfie was staggering towards a chair to support himself, his face full of naked pain.

I had a feeling he wasn't going to be Bertie Wooster after all.

13

In which Rags has her suspicions about Hengist confirmed

As I drove away I asked myself who could have snatched the part of Bertie Wooster away from Alfie. The answer came to me in a flash: it must have been the scruffy young man. There had been no one else of the right age sitting in that circle in the church hall. I wondered where he'd sprung from, and whether Hengist had head-hunted him from another am dram company, believing that Alfie wasn't up to delivering a performance that would secure the treasured prize in the competition.

Then, before I reached my flat, I caught sight of something very interesting indeed.

I'd turned off the road to Holkham and was driving towards Freeman Street when I saw Janette jump out of a car parked at the entrance of the track that led across the fields to Pinewoods Holiday Park. Though she was wearing a shapeless woolly hat, with her hair tucked up beneath it, a few golden strands trailing down her back and her profile made her recognisable. I slowed to a halt and in my rear view mirror watched the car, a black Audi, pull on to the road and head away from the coast. Hengist was at the wheel. Janette hurried through the rain towards the coast.

'Janette!' I wound down my window. 'Can I give you a lift?'

Her step faltered then she came over to me with the determined smile on her face that I was beginning to associate with all those who had dealings with Hengist. 'I'm fine, thanks. I only live down there,' she said, indicating a side road a hundred metres ahead.

'Jump in.' I opened the passenger side door. 'You'll get soaked if you walk.'

After a short hesitation, she got into the car. I followed her directions until we pulled up outside a small house. Instead of jumping out of the car, she sat there, looking straight ahead.

'I was just talking to Hengist about my part,' she said, after a few moments to gather her thoughts. 'He's got some ideas he wants me to pursue.'

I nodded, pretty sure he'd had a few other things he wanted to pursue with her. 'Don't say anything to anyone, will you? I don't want to it get back to Jem.'

'I promise I won't say a word.'

'Only he's a bit sensitive about Hengist. I've told him our relationship is strictly professional, but he sometimes gets these ideas.'

I assured her again that I'd say nothing to Jem or anyone else. At this, the tension left her body and she turned to me with a genuine smile.

'Getting the part of Madeline Bassett is a dream come true. Hengist knows an agent in London who's going to come and see the production. He says she's bound to sign me up.'

'That's fantastic news.'

'And then I want to get into television. That's where the money is.'

'Well I wish you all the luck in the world.'

'Thanks.'

I expected her to get out of the car, but she sat there a little longer, the smell of wet wool from her purple knitted hat filling the car. 'Most people round here have got no ambition,' she said. 'They just want to do a boring job, get married and settle down. But I want more than that. I want to make something of myself.'

'And Jem?' I asked gently.

She laughed – an easy, charming laugh. 'Jem'll do anything I tell him. He's a good carpenter and will always be able to find work. He can support me in between acting jobs.'

'You seem to have it all figured out.'

'I have.' A shadow flitted over her young, hopeful face. 'I just had to get the part of Madeline Bassett.' She turned to look at me, the humour gone from her big blue eyes. 'You understand, don't you?'

'Yes,' I said, remembering the hot ambition that had coursed through me when I was in my twenties. 'But be careful,' I couldn't help adding. 'Don't compromise your principles.'

A shutter came down over her face. 'Thanks for the lift,' she called, wriggling out of the car.

I watched her run up the path to a front door in need of a lick of paint. In a few seconds she was gone.

My phone rang. Dad.

'Hi Dad. I've been meaning to call. How are things?'

'Good.' I heard him take an anxious breath. 'I've been wondering how things are going with your mother.'

'Fine,' I said. 'She's no bother – no bother at all. In fact

I've hardly seen her.'

His relief ran down the phone line. 'Well, that's good to hear. I know you were excited about getting your own flat, and her turning up like that was a bit of a shock.'

'Don't worry, Dad. It's all being taken care of.'

'Have you heard from Nigel?'

'No.'

'But I expect he'll be in touch soon, won't he?'

'Yes. I'm sure he will.'

We were both silent with our thoughts for a while before Dad spoke again. 'Do you fancy a walk? Napoleon would love a run in the beach. I know it's raining but ...'

'I'd love that.'

When I got into the flat I found a note pinned to the door.

In small, purple script it read: 'I've received a beautiful invitation. Not sure when I'll be home. Gwendolyn.'

What the dickens was she up to now?

Oh well. She was a grown-up and could look after herself.

I pulled on some walking boots, dug out a light mac, and changed into a pair of comfortable jeans and a loose cotton sweater. Its pale blue reminded me of days under cloudless skies spent paddling in warm waves then eating ice creams at Wells when I was a kid – the sort of magical day that only came along a few times a year, when Dad was able to tear himself away from Gwendolyn and take me to the coast, leaving her to sulk over her palmistry magazines in our dingy terraced house on the outskirts of Kings Lynn.

Dad's parents had grown up in Wells and his childhood summers were spent on the quay and at the beach. The heavy air of defeat that hung around him like a shroud when we were at home lifted as we took the curves of the coast road.

When we hit the flint-faced pub and estate buildings of Holkham he'd turn to me and say, 'Nearly there, Raggy. I bet you can't wait.' And, no, I couldn't wait: by then I was fidgeting and longing to breathe the air of the harbour and the salt marsh.

The rain was subsiding by the time Dad picked me up near the Albatros – the cargo ship with the lofty masts once leased to Greenpeace and now a bar and restaurant moored on the quay. We motored down to Pinewoods in his Mini, with Napoleon perched on my knee. After we'd parked, Napoleon scooted ahead of us to the gate and sandy path that ran through the woods. Hoods up, we strolled beside the boating lake, watching a few ducks making silvery ripples on the water's surface. I took a deep breath, savouring the scent of pine and damp earth.

As we walked we chatted about this and that. Dad asked me if I'd got started on the costumes for *Jeeves Pulls it Off*, and I told him about Toots inviting me for raspberries and cream. He laughed. 'You'll enjoy spending time with her.'

I told Dad I thought Alfie had probably missed out on the part of Bertie Wooster. He tutted. 'Oh, that's a shame. I know he'd got his heart set on it.'

'But it's great that Janette's got the part she wanted, isn't it?'

Dad's face cleared. 'Yes. She's a lovely girl. No side to her, and properly talented.'

As we climbed the wooden walkway that led to the beach I brought Dad up to date with my investigation into Zillah's disappearance. 'I wish you'd met her, Dad. I'd love to know what you make of her.'

'Go on.'

'You see, they found stuff associated with drug taking

in her flat – syringes, a bag with a few grains of powder in it, a blackened spoon – all the stuff that goes with taking opiates. But no one who knows her believes that she was interested in any sort of drugs, let alone the hard stuff. I can't work it out.'

Dad looked thoughtful. 'People have secrets. When you talked to her, did you think she was hiding anything from you?'

I ran over my meeting with Zillah in my mind. 'Yes. Yes, I think she was, but I don't think it had anything to do with drugs.'

We started our descent down the wooden steps that led to the beach huts and the huge expanse of beach. Napoleon emerged out of the undergrowth with a stick as long as his body and dropped it at my feet. I picked it up, threw it and watched his body bounce across the sand in pursuit.

'And how are things going with your mother?'

'She's hardly there, and when she is, we keep out of each other's way,' I replied, deciding not to burden Dad with Gwendolyn's statement that we were both earthbound cynics. 'She seems to be OK.'

'Well that's a relief.'

At the foot of the steps we started to walk towards the sea, enjoying the rhythmic music of waves breaking far out, and the gleam of the channels winding towards the shore. As we headed towards the dunes that sat between the coast and the sea he talked about Susie – how they were planning a long weekend away in The Lake District in October and were looking for an AirBnB that welcomed dogs. A little knife ran through my heart. I wanted to look for an AirBnB. I wanted to go away with a lover and be soppy beside a lake.

But there was no sign of that at the moment.

14

***In which we meet Hugh Blackthorn and
The Peasmarsh Players prepare to rehearse***

Hugh Blackthorn

At the sound of the clanking tea trolley the Reverend Hugh Blackthorn prised his eyes open and reached for a drink of water from the bedside cabinet. Ouch. His head throbbed every time he moved, but at least he was fully conscious and in possession of his wits again.

He'd been in hospital for nearly a week. He'd drifted in and out of consciousness for a couple of days, and been kept in for observation after that because his mind had been a sickly fog.

He can't recall exactly what happened the night he was injured. He knows that he had something important to do, but he can't quite recall what it was. He's rummaged around in his murky mind, but he can't remember anything after four o'clock, when he left the parish office after working on his Sunday sermon.

He's not even sure who's been to visit him in hospital, though he thinks Evangeline has come more than once – Evangeline, who's been in love with him for years, despite marrying the hopeless Terry. Mrs Grace, the pinched church warden, certainly put in an appearance and he was ashamed to admit he'd kept his eyes shut and his hearing aid switched off so he didn't have to listen to her droning on about the poor quality of Evangeline's flower arrangements. 'They're so *common*. Positively funereal.'

Well, Evangeline's flower arrangements were a bit stiff and forbidding, but she'd been a loyal friend to the church, and he wasn't going to listen to Mrs Grace running her down.

The one person he really wanted to see hadn't come.

Zillah. Beautiful Zillah, with her grey eyes and hair fine as silk. All he wanted to do was hold her hand, listen to her voice. But she hadn't turned up at the hospital. Oh, he'd forgotten lots of things, but he knew he would have remembered that.

He sighed. He hadn't really expected her to come. Coming into Norwich could be dangerous: someone might recognise her. And that someone might tell The Sistren and then her mother would come looking for her. Her horrible, cold-hearted mother. He'd been outraged when he heard what Julie – he wouldn't grace her with the name of Saint Julian of Norwich – had put Zillah through. The poor child had been imprisoned for years. If he ever met Julie face to face, he'd give her a piece of his mind.

A voice broke into his festering thoughts. 'Here's your tea, love. Would you like a biscuit?'

He opened his eyes to see Vera, the kind-hearted volunteer tea lady with a face wrinkled into soft folds and crannies by the forty fags a day she'd smoked for sixty years. She was smiling at him – they all smiled at him since they'd found out that he was a vicar, and he felt obliged to smile back, even when he didn't feel like smiling.

'Thank you, Vera. That would be lovely.'

She dished out two Hob-nobs and then, with a wink, added one extra. 'To build up your strength,' she whispered bending so close he could smell the hair spray and smoke in her hair.

'You spoil me.'

She drew back, with a cackle, her bright blue eyes dancing with laughter. A grin broke over his face. He loved old women like her, full of mischief and optimism. They were a lesson to him. With a contented sigh he reached for his tea – hot and strong, just as he liked it. Outside the sun was wrestling with the rain clouds that had lowered over the hospital all day. It would break through soon.

A faint sense of optimism crept into his aching head. He'd been told he'd be discharged later that day: Evangeline was coming to collect him and said he could stay with her overnight. He was grateful for that, since he still felt a bit shaky.

When he got back to St Botolph's he'd be able to talk to Zillah. There were things he needed to discuss with her – to sort out.

Once and for all.

* *

Janette Tinker

Janette hurried in her front door, kicking off her uncomfortable high heels and undoing the buttons on her flowery cotton dress (short enough to show plenty of leg) as she made for the bathroom. Here she turned on the shower, pulled off the push-up bra she only wore when she *had* to and the sensible knickers that creepy man was never going to see, and ducked under the stream of water. It was only luke-warm, but she didn't care. She just needed to wash off the taint of that man's fingers, the smell of his cologne.

Thank goodness Mum was at work: she'd have known something was up. But Mum was on another double-shift at the care home, making some extra cash so Janette could buy something nice for when the agent from London came to see her in the play.

And Jem was away in Sussex for a few days, doing the joinery on the renovation of a huge house for a couple of bankers. She was glad he wasn't here: it was easier to get on with what she had to do when he wasn't around.

As the water trickled through her hair, Janette told herself it wasn't so bad. She hadn't done anything she hadn't done before. She'd learned since she was twelve that there were ways of getting things out of men – drinks, meals, gifts, lifts – and nothing too terrible had happened to her.

Shivering, she turned off the water and dried herself with a towel that had seen better days. After she'd dressed in baggy track-suit bottoms and a fleece she sat herself down with her script and ran through the lines of the first act of *Jeeves Pulls it Off*. As she did, she could feel her body relaxing. This was all she wanted to do, all she wanted to be. And she could feel in her gut that she was going to make it – and not just in an amateur production in Wells-next-the-Sea. The agent would sign her up. She'd move to London, and within a couple of years would get her big break. She'd stopped telling Jem this, as he always laughed and told her not to be too carried away. But she knew. She just *knew*.

A ping from her phone jolted her out of Madeline Bassett's cosy world.

She shook her head. Sad sack. Then she texted a reply, finishing with a smiley emoji.

Love to. Just tell me where and when. ☺ xxx

* *

Hengist Bright

In his pristine study, Hengist perused the cast list for *Jeeves Pulls it Off*, making a few neat notes beside the main characters:

Bertie Wooster: Iain Bright – Check he's up to date with learning lines.
Jeeves: Cedric Williams – Appearance? Grooming?
Madeline Bassett: Janette Tinker – One-to-one sessions?
Gussie Fink-Nottle: Dave Bennett – Could be sharper.
Aunt Agatha: Betzy Stretch – Minimum contact.

There. All things considered, he was satisfied with his cast. Iain would make an excellent Bertie Wooster, though he'd had a hell of a job persuading him to take the role. Cedric would be fabulous as Jeeves. Ditto Janette as Madeline Bassett. Dave was not the strongest actor, but he'd put in a solid performance. Betzy was a cold fish, suited down to the ground to play the caustic, domineering Aunt Agatha: she even had the beaky nose and haughty demeanour. But he intended to keep his distance: her claws were sharp.

He turned to his copy of the script, marking it up with stage directions and editorial notes ready for the first rehearsal that evening.

Thank heavens that idiot Alfie wouldn't ruin the production this time. He wasn't a bad actor, but always managed to screw things up. He'd made a laughing stock of them all when he'd forgotten to turn up for his entrance in the final act of *All My Sons*. And in the production before that, of an Alan Bennett play, Alfie had tripped over a rug and gone flat on the floor. The boy was a walking disaster. Hengist would have got shot of him a long time ago if his doting mother hadn't kept donating considerable sums to the Players with heavy hints that her generosity would end if Alfie wasn't given a starring role. Well, probate was finally through on Mindy's father's estate, and he and Mindy were now sitting on a large pile of cash. He didn't need to placate Alfie's mother, or anyone else for that matter.

From the lawn outside came a stifled yelp. Getting up from his chair, he strolled to the window to take a look. Beckett, his wife's smooth-haired Visla, was perched with his backside hovering a centimetre above the ground and Mindy was walking away from him. About twenty metres further on she stopped and turned around. Beckett squirmed but didn't move. Mindy lifted one hand and called, 'Come!' With a bark of pleasure, the dog leapt up and pounded towards her over the closely mown lawn. When he reached her, Beckett sidled round until he was sitting close to her right foot. With a hint of a smile, Mindy reached into her pocket and brought out a couple of treats for him.

Pushing the window open, Hengist called, 'Brilliant! If you carry on like this you'll walk the obedience class at the Hunstanton show.'

She waved at him then bent down to stroke Beckett's satiny ears. The Visla had been a manic puppy when she got him a year before, but Mindy wasn't a woman to be defeated by a dog, and she'd now got him trained to perfection.

Ah, but she hasn't quite managed to train me, thought Hengist as he closed the window and returned to his desk.

Speaking of which ... he unlocked his desk drawer and pulled out a phone. Mindy was leaving the house in an hour, on her way to a consultancy job in Budapest. And while she was gone ...

Perhaps he'd arrange to meet up with Janette outside of rehearsal time. She was inexperienced but had the makings of an excellent actress and would respond to extra coaching.

He would have cast her as Madeline Bassett in any case, but the twit was so eager to get the part that she'd agreed to do a little something for him.

And he needed to check that everything was going to plan.

Then a sudden thought struck him: he needed to get into the church hall and Hugh wasn't around. Bugger. He'd have to talk to Evangeline, the dreadful battleaxe who guarded Hugh's kingdom as if it were Buckingham Palace. With a groan he pulled his iPhone from his pocket and dialled the parish office. Fortunately she picked up, as graceless as usual.

'I'll leave the hall unlocked, and you can put the key through the office letterbox when you've finished.'

And cut him off.

Charming.

* *

Cedric Williams

After leaving a long, apologetic message, Cedric hung up. With a groan he cracked his knuckles. He hoped that did the trick. People could be so *unreasonable.* He was caught between a rock and a hard place.

Speaking of which, his wife Sheila was coming up the stairs. Hastily he slipped the phone into his jeans pocket and bent over his laptop, pretending to work.

'Oo-ooh! Can I come in?'

Before he could answer, she barged in the door, wielding a pair of nifty hairdresser's scissors and a towel.

'I thought I'd give you a trim before you head off tonight. You really *can't* go like that, darling.' She tossed the towel round his neck, fastened it with a peg, and pulled a comb out of her pocket. 'It'll only take two ticks, and then you'll be ready to knock 'em dead.'

Her cheerful voice grated on him. Oh, if only he had the guts to tell her to sod off and leave him alone.

But once she'd decided on something there was no stopping her. He'd just have to put up with it.

With firm hands she raked the comb through his hair, snagging on his ear so that he yelped. 'Oh don't be a baby!' she cried, starting to snip away at the grey wisps curling over his collar. Resigned, he watched her tidy up his hair until he looked less of a scruff and more of a Jeeves. Grudgingly he admitted that she made a good job of it – among her many other skills, she'd learned how to cut hair when the girls were young – and since he was going to have to do this bloody production, he might as well look the part.

'There.' Bending down, she planted a loud kiss on the top of his head. 'I can get the clippers out nearer show time, to give you a totally authentic look.'

'Thank you,' he mumbled, hating the way he sounded like a bad-tempered teen.

'My pleasure, darling!' she chirped. 'Cheer up! It might never happen.'

Oh but it might. It would. Sooner or later it would.

15

In which Rags attends the first rehearsal of Jeeves Pulls it Off

I took it easy on the afternoon before the first rehearsal of *Jeeves Pulls it Off*. There was nothing more I could do about Zillah's disappearance for the time being and Gwendolyn was off somewhere attending to spiritual matters, so I had the flat to myself.

I read for a while – one of the novels on the Women's Prize shortlist picked up from the library – then picked up my guitar. It was a while since I'd played – I'd been too busy, too distracted. But nothing is more satisfying than running through a few songs. I turned to my Joni Mitchell repertoire – *Carey*, *A Case of You*, and *Big Yellow Taxi* – and cursed my way through some bar chord practice. The chord of F hadn't got any easier in the week during which I'd not touched my guitar. At about 5.30 I had a shower and prepared a meal of salad and new potatoes.

Fortified, I headed off to meet Toots, who'd promised to show me a way to walk on footpaths to Peasmarsh.

The day had mellowed into a fine, warm evening as Toots led me to a path that started in a meadow, telling me that in March and April it was full of hares. 'I'd like to get my hands on those bastards who go out shooting them,' she said, narrowing her eyes.

'I couldn't agree more,' I said, remembering how during my last investigation I'd learned about the men (and it was only men) who went lamping in the fields surrounding the Holkham Estate, driving their cars into fields, turning the headlights on full, then shooting the startled hares.

'Come on. Race you to the stile,' called Toots. Surprisingly swift, she set off at a smart pace and just about beat me to the end of the field, where we both clutched our midriffs and caught our breath. She grinned at me. 'You wouldn't believe it to look at me now, but I was 400-metre runner when I was in my teens.'

'The only running I did was for the school bus.'

Once over the stile, we pottered on towards the spire of St Botolph's piercing a sky filled with gauzy light. Ten minutes later we were in the hall, where some of the cast were already milling around, making teas and coffees. There was still half an hour to go before the start of the rehearsal – the cast had been asked to get there early to be measured up – and the first to come over was Cedric, the actor playing Jeeves. He'd smartened up since I last saw him: his hair had been trimmed and his clothes were tidier. But he still seemed tense and less than happy to have the honour of playing Jeeves handed to him. 'You should know my vital statistics by now,' he said, making an effort to be pleasant as Toots ran the tape measure round various parts of his anatomy.

'You'd be surprised how much people can change in six months,' she said, jotting down figures in her notebook. 'Anyway, how are things?'

Cedric's jaw clenched before he rallied. 'They're fine. My new book is coming along well.'

'Cedric's an author,' said Toots, 'a famous author.'

A slight blush rose into Cedric's face. 'I wouldn't say I was famous.'

'But your last book was up for a prize, wasn't it?'

'What was it about?' I asked.

'The Beat Poets and their contemporaries in Britain.'

'Wow. Sounds really interesting.' I'd never managed to write a whole book, though I'd threatened to do so throughout my twenties.

His appreciative smile was genuine, but there was a strain of sadness behind it, and I wondered where that came from. 'What are you working on now?'

'A book about the Pointillist painters.' He gave a self-deprecating laugh. 'I like to tackle group biographies – to capture the social milieu of artists and writers as well as individual lives.'

I scrabbled in my bag for a business card giving my contact details. 'I'm a journalist. Let me know if you decide to have a book launch and I'll see if I can help you get some media coverage.'

His face relaxed a fraction. 'Thank you.'

As soon as we'd finished and he'd wandered off to take his place in the circle for the read-through, Toots leant over to speak softly in my ear: 'He's a sweetheart married to a right-wing bigot. I don't know how he stands it.'

I had a pretty good idea. Authors, even those short-listed for prizes, seldom earn above minimum wage. I suspected his wife was the one who kept him afloat.

Janette was next for the tape measure. 'Same as last time,' said Toots. 'Haven't changed an inch – or a centimetre.'

I noticed that she wasn't quite her usual bubbly self. Remembering that I'd promised to say nothing about her tryst (if that's what it was) with Hengist, I said nothing. As she left to take her place in the circle, she shot me a grateful smile.

Dave appeared, wearing horn-rimmed spectacles and a tweed jacket. 'I'm getting in the Fink-Nottle zone,' he said, winking at me before pulling off his jacket so Toots could measure his chest. I winked back, thinking how nice it was to be *flirted* with again.

Betzy Stretch, the woman playing Aunt Agatha, was one of those athletic, rangy women who look as if they'd come out on top in a pub brawl.

'Same as before,' said Toots, with an approving smile, when she'd finished measuring.

'It just takes a little discipline.'

I watched her stalk off to her chair. She should have been everything I admired – a strong, no-nonsense woman who pandered to no one – but she had a chilly vibe I didn't trust. 'She's an odd fish,' I whispered to Toots.

'Made a packet in the city then moved up here a few years ago. She's down the gym every day, building up her biceps.'

Before we could gossip further, Hengist arrived, looking suave in black jeans and shirt, and called everyone into the circle.

'First of all, can I introduce you to our Bertie?' said Hengist, gesturing to the young man by his side. 'I'm delighted to say that Iain will be joining us for this production. We'll start with a read-through of Act One.'

Toots suggested we measure Iain for his costume during the break, and she and I dragged a couple of chairs into the circle to listen to the read-through.

Ah, the genius of P G Wodehouse. My parents had never been fans, but at university a very dear, very camp pal, had introduced me to the novels. The play was not quite the real thing, but it was fun, and Cedric was brilliant as Jeeves. He caught perfectly the fact that Jeeves is 100 times more intelligent than Bertie, but has a sense of decorum and basic kindness that never leads him to humiliate his employer. Iain, the young man playing Bertie, who'd arrived too late for us to take his measurements, was pretty damn good, too.

At about quarter to nine the cast took a break. Toots got out her tape measure while I jotted down the figures for Iain's costume, after which we decided to head back to Wells – this time on the road, as it was getting dark. As we left I saw Cedric take a call on his phone, flinching as he rushed from the hall to speak to whoever was calling. Toots and I raised eyebrows at each other. 'Probably his wife,' she mouthed at me.

After a stroll through the gathering dusk we hit the Eddie at about twenty past nine and got stuck into discussing the evening.

'Iain – the guy cast as Bertie – was good wasn't he?'

Toots raised her eyebrows.

'What?'

'He's Hengist's son. I could see you wondering where on earth he'd sprung from.'

'Has he been in other productions?'

'When he was a teenager. But he's been off the scene for a few years, doing his A-levels then at university. I think he's just graduated.' She took a sip of her wine. 'He seems to have had a major change of heart. The last time, I saw him, at the after-show party for *The Importance of Being Earnest*, I overheard him talking to Hengist, and I think his actual words were, 'You're a fucking control freak. I'm never going to act in one of your sad productions again.'

'Then why's he agreed to take on the role of Bertie Wooster?'

'Search me.'

Right on cue, Alfie Adams, the actor who'd have given his right arm to play Bertie Wooster, wandered in the door of the pub, looking rather more haggard than when I'd last seen him at Blue Sky Cottages. He said a quick hello then hurried to the bar, where he ordered a double vodka and tonic, downed it in a few gulps, and ordered another.

'Someone's drowning his sorrows,' I said quietly to Toots.

'I feel for him. Hengist strung him along for weeks. I'm not surprised he's gutted.'

Alfie had been joined by a friend – a man about his own age with a floppy blonde fringe, and as they talked, Alfie's loud, drunken voice carried to our quiet table.

'I could fucking *kill* him.'

16

In which Rags drinks coffee with Gwendolyn again

The next morning I was again woken up by the smell of coffee. I could hear Gwendolyn moving around the kitchen, and singing quietly. Listening hard, I identified *The Circle Game*, the old Joni Mitchell song – or rather, a version of it, since Gwendolyn can't sing for toffee. She's one of the twenty-per-cent of the human race who has no sense of pitch. Dad and I, on the other hand, can sing and harmonise without difficulty. Hearing Gwendolyn murdering Joni's song reminded me that I should have a go at it on my guitar, now I'd started practising again.

I reached for my phone: just after seven. Not too bad. I'd got in from the pub at eleven and gone straight to bed, instead of turning on the TV as I usually did. Having Gwendolyn in residence upstairs prevented me from watching too much on the box: I didn't want to wake her, not just out of consideration but also because I didn't want to encourage her to come downstairs for a mother-daughter bonding session.

But that was childish. I couldn't avoid her forever.

Throwing back the covers, I padded into the kitchen, determined to have a civil conversation – a conversation between two adults.

When I opened the door she had her back to me. 'Good morning,' I called.

She turned, her face lit up with sun. 'Good morning to you! I hope I didn't wake you.'

Something about the joy in her face plucked at my heart strings. 'You seem happy.'

'I am.' She gave a rueful smile that made her look much younger than her years. 'I feel as if I've found my spiritual home. I never want to leave.'

Never?

'Have you been in touch with Nigel?' I asked. 'Only I feel the two of you should talk.'

She waved this away with a hand that looked suspiciously like it had just had an expensive manicure. 'All in good time. We're in different places, spiritually speaking. But for now I'm enjoying spending time with my beautiful daughter.' She paused to give me another radiant smile. 'Coffee?'

'Yes, please.'

She poured us each a small cup and held one out to me. 'Here.'

I helped myself to sugar and a dash of milk, and we both sat down at the table. As we sipped I asked myself if she was just putting on a brave face.

'So how are you feeling?' I asked.

'Me? Fine. I'm sleeping like a baby.'

'About Nigel. How are you feeling about him? You must be hurt by what he's done.'

She looked down into her coffee, then up at me with serious eyes. 'Hurt and pain only arise when you're too attached to people and things.'

This seemed a little simplistic when talking about a thirty-year marriage, but I let it go, saying instead, 'So, you've found like-minded souls in North Norfolk?'

The smile returned to her face. 'I certainly have.' She wagged a finger at me. 'But I'm not going to tell you any more than that, because you'll make fun of me.'

'No, I won't!' I said, suppressing a bristle at that wagging finger.

'Oh yes you will. I know you think my spiritual beliefs are clap-trap ...'

'No, I don't!'

'... and I'm not going to open myself up to your ridicule.'

Rebuked, I sat in silence as she stood up and rinsed our cups. I took a deep breath, determined to continue with this adult conversation thing. 'I'm sorry if I've made fun of your beliefs in the past, but I really am interested in what's going on for you at the moment.'

Gwendolyn ran her fingers through her hair, checking her appearance in the little mirror I'd tacked up on the wall beside the sink. 'Are you serious?' she said, without turning round.

'Yes.'

She returned to the table, eyes gleaming. 'I've been exploring past lives.'

I gave a slight nod, to show that I was listening.

'You'd be amazed at how far I've travelled.' She leant forward, close enough for me to see each false eyelash. 'I'm sure I was an Indian princess in an earlier life. I could smell the sacred waters of the Ganges.'

I almost cracked a joke about how you could smell the sacred waters of the Ganges from miles away because of the raw sewage floating in it.

'And ... and I know that you were a warrior in the Dark Ages – a female warrior, like – what's her name? – Boadicea. Queen of the Saxons.'

Boudicca, Queen of the Iceni, I was itching to say, but didn't.

'You were dressed in a tunic and carrying a spear and driving a chariot. It was so *thrilling*.'

'Wow.' I was quite enjoying this.

'Of course your father was an illiterate peasant.'

'What?'

Her face lost its dreamy look. 'You heard. And don't scowl at me like that: I can't control what visions the spirits bring.'

'Dad was never a peasant,' I spat, surprised at the extent of the anger that had reared up inside me. 'He's smart and he's educated. Did you know that he's been taking online history courses? And getting great marks?'

The last bit was a fib, as his assignments weren't marked, but I'd read them and they were seriously good, and I wasn't going to let Gwendolyn slag him off.

She stood up abruptly. 'I knew you wouldn't understand.'

'At least I'm interested in the real world and real events.' Then, as she stormed out of the room, 'And Boadicea lived during the Roman occupation of Britain and not the Dark Ages! And she was called Boudicca!'

I sat there, listening to her footsteps running up the stairs to the bedroom, already regretting my hasty words. She'd had a go at Dad, and yet again I'd acted like a little kid. I heard her footsteps again and a moment later she poked her head round the living-room door, a large canvas bag slung over her shoulder. 'I was talking about your father in a past incarnation. Surely even you can see that.'

'Yeah – a past incarnation in which he's a peasant.'

'And what's wrong with being a peasant? I thought you were all for social equality and equal rights.'

I took a breath but couldn't find the right words, and knew I'd over-reacted. 'Look, Mum,' I started, 'I'm sorry

I ...'

'I've told you not to call me that!' she barked. 'And don't wait up for me. I don't know when I'll be back.'

She slammed the door behind her and ran down the stairs to the street.

Oh crap.

I paced the room for a little while, then made myself another cup of coffee and retreated to the sofa bed to distract myself by reading *Curlew Moon*, by Mary Colwell – a wonderful book Toots had lent me about the plight of these beautiful, long-beaked birds. Since returning to Norfolk I'd got more in touch with the natural world – its beauties and the way it was threatened. Inspired by watching curlews poke their long beaks into the muddy salt marsh on my strolls along the coastal path towards Cley, I was thinking of pitching a couple of features about bird conservation to wildlife magazines. Writing about curlews was a more appealing prospect than churning out another article along the lines of *Keeping your Mojo after Menopause*. These features, written under my daft pseudonym of Bee Cool, had kept me afloat after I was sacked from my last proper job as a journalist, but I was bored to the back teeth of them now.

The ringing of my phone pulled me out of Colwell's account of the dismal decline of curlews in Ireland. I picked it up: Dad, his voice breathless and agitated.

'Turn on the local news. Hengist has been found dead – possibly murdered.'

17

In which Rags finds that St Botolph's churchyard can be a dangerous place

I rushed to turn on the TV, catching the tail-end of the broadcast from St Botolph's churchyard.

Detective Inspector Chloe Cooper was speaking – the same DI with whom I'd had a few run-ins earlier in the year. I pulled a face: she'd not been the most helpful police officer, and I was not looking forward to dealing with her again, if I found out anything that needed to be reported to the police.

'The police are keen to talk to anyone who saw Hengist Bright after the rehearsal of The Peasmarsh Players last night. We know that he was safe and well at ten o'clock, at the end of the rehearsal held in the church hall, but at some time later that night he was attacked by an assailant wielding a piece of stone from a broken gravestone. His body was found in St Botolph's churchyard early this morning. If you can provide any information, please ring 101 to arrange to talk to an officer, or visit Wells-next-the-Sea police station, where an incident room has been set up.'

Dad was talking again. 'I just want to know that you're all right. It sounds like there's some sort of maniac on the loose in that village.'

I assured him that I was fine, adding, 'I doubt that it's a maniac. Hengist had rubbed a lot of people up the wrong way, and it's possible he got into a serious dispute with someone that got out of hand.'

'But what about Hugh? Perhaps he was attacked as well.'

He had a point; one serious head injury and one death in less than a week were unlikely to be a coincidence. 'I don't know, Dad. Perhaps you're right.'

He sighed. 'Ah well. I can't say I took to Hengist, but what a dreadful thing to happen to him.'

Soon after he rang off a small miracle happened: a text came in saying that BT Openworld would definitely come to connect my landline and broadband that afternoon, between 12 and 4.

At least *something* good had come to pass.

Motivated by the prospect of having broadband, I decided to spend some time on an overdue Bee Cool feature I'd promised Tabby, the features editor at *All Woman*. Titled, *Dipping your Toe in the Water*, it was about the erotic possibilities of feet and toes. They're not really my bag: though I love a good foot rub, I don't want someone licking or sucking my toes. No, thank you.

But Bee Cool had promised to crank out 2,000 words on the subject, so I put my personal reservations on the back burner. I'd already downloaded some stuff on my laptop last time I was at Dad's, so I spent a couple of hours distracting myself by putting together a feature that focussed on giving feet some serious TLC, and using them as a part of intimate contact. Through reading around I discovered that a foot fetish is usually safe and affectionate, and I was gratified to discover that those who found feet erotic usually hated the corns and callouses as much as I did.

Julian, Zillah's mother, rang just as I was putting the finishing touches to the piece. 'I need to talk to you. The police have been on to me. They're looking for Zillah. And I'm sure they suspect her of murder. Can we meet up?'

I asked her to come over to my place, since I wasn't going to miss my chance to finally get hooked up to broadband. She readily agreed. Just over an hour later she was ringing the doorbell. I ran downstairs and invited her in. Dressed as before in her shapeless oatmeal sack, her face was thinner, more drawn.

Julian explained that the police had visited her at The Sistren House that morning, asking questions about Zillah's whereabouts.

'I told them I'd heard nothing from her since she left the House eight weeks ago. Have you made any progress with finding where she's been since she left St Botolph's?'

I shook my head.

She took a deep breath. 'Well they're pretty certain she was at the church yesterday evening, threatening the man who died.'

'That doesn't sound like Zillah.'

Julian opened her mouth as if to say something, then pressed her lips together again.

'What? Please tell me. If I'm to help you, I need to know everything.'

After a bit of a tussle with herself, she got the words out. 'Zillah did have some anger issues when she was a teenager.'

'What sort of issues?'

'She was furious when I forbade her to see Tracey, but Tracey was idle, vain and sex-mad. When they were together the two of them spent all their time giggling and talking about boys. It was immoral.'

It sounded completely normal to me, but I bit my tongue, reminding myself that I was working for Julian, and needed to put my personal antipathy to one side.

'But her anger issues were resolved years ago by prayer and meditation. She's now a perfectly well adjusted young woman.'

I somehow doubted that: after years in a cult, it would be a miracle if Zillah hadn't been affected in some way, despite her composed exterior.

'I know my daughter is not a murderer and I want you to find out who did this. To prove her innocence.'

I agreed to carry on with my investigation, adding that my fee would be the same as before. Yes, the money would be welcome, but more important than that, I agreed with Julian on one thing.

I didn't believe Zillah had murdered Hengist.

18

In which Rags draws up a list of suspects

No sooner had Julian left than BT Openworld arrived to set up my broadband. The engineer was in and out within ten minutes. Wahoo! After all the stressing out, I was now fully connected.

I had a pretty good idea who'd seen Zillah at the church: Bert, the friend of Edward, the elderly man I'd met in the churchyard the morning after Hugh Blackthorn was injured. He'd told me that Bert lived in the sheltered housing complex adjoining the church and kept a close eye on the goings-on at St Botolph's.

I decided he'd be more willing to talk to me if I came with someone he knew, so rang Edward. He was delighted to hear from me again, and readily agreed to set up a meeting with Bert, adding, 'We could be a team, like that Cagney and Lacey on the television.' That made me smile, as I was pretty certain the series ended at least 30 years ago. I had misty memories of watching it on the TV as a little kid.

While I was waiting for Edward to call me back with a time to meet Bert, I started a preliminary list of suspects.

1. *Alfie Adams* – *bitterly disappointed at not getting the part of Bertie Wooster and broadcasted the fact that he wanted to kill Hengist.*

2. *Jem Townley* – *jealous of Hengist, and probably suspected him of demanding sexual favours from Janette.*

3. *Mindy Bright* – *might have found out about Hengist's serial infidelity. Though she was travelling to Budapest on the night Hengist was killed, she could have arranged for someone to murder him.*

4. *Janette Tinker* – *I was sure Hengist had involved her in some sort of sexual activity as a reward for giving her the part that would help her achieve her dream to become a professional actor. Did she seek revenge?*

5. *Zillah Lloyd* – *seen arguing with Hengist after the rehearsal. A history of rages when younger.*

6. *An unknown person* – *perhaps a woman who'd had an unsavoury encounter with Hengist in the past, or had fallen in love with him and couldn't stand being rejected when he insisted on staying with Mindy.*

Of these six (so far) possible murderers, I thought Jem was the most likely culprit. Janette had told me that he was jealous of Hengist, and he easily had the strength to kill someone by hitting them on the head with a piece of gravestone. Alfie was probably just shooting his mouth off: we all say we could kill someone, but we don't mean it, literally. On the other hand, when Toots and I saw him he was clearly set on getting blind drunk, and might have attacked Hengist while he was out of his head. I shut my eyes for a moment, trying to recall if he'd been in the Eddie for the whole evening. Nope. I was pretty certain he'd vanished long before closing time.

As for Hengist's wife, Mindy, she was flying to Budapest on the night he was killed, but she was a cool customer who had the brains to set up something like this. Toots had hinted that she had a vengeful nature. What if she'd decided to punish Hengist?

I thought Janette was unlikely to have murdered Hengist because he was her ticket to getting an agent.

And as for Zillah, I hoped against hope that she hadn't killed Hengist, and intended to look hard for an alternative prime suspect. But why had she been arguing with Hengist?

The phone rang: Edward, saying Bert was happy to meet us, and was free that afternoon.

'Could we head over to Peasmarsh now?'

'I don't see why not. I'll meet you at St Botolph's in half an hour. OK, partner?'

'OK.'

Before I left the house I proof-read *Dipping your Toe in the Water* and sent it off. It wasn't Nobel-prize-winning stuff, but it would have to do.

Bert was a tall man with a large moon of a face. Whereas Edward was wiry and quick in his movements and thoughts, Bert was ponderous. His face sagged and wrinkled as he thought of what to say and how to say it. He had a kindness about him that was echoed by the way he stroked the large black and white cat (Piebald) sitting on his lap. Before I asked him about the goings-on at St Botolph's we sat with Earl Grey tea and Garibaldi biscuits and chatted for a while. He told me that he'd lost his wife, Phyllis, a long time ago. 'She died when our Andrea was only ten,' he said, pointing at a photograph of their wedding day propped up on the mantelpiece. Bert looked pin-sharp in suit and tie, and Phyllis was radiant in a meringue of a dress, complete with veil.

'21st of June 1960. Soon after that Phyllis found she was expecting so it was fortunate I had my job in the bank – National Provincial it was then.'

'She looks beautiful.'

'She was, wasn't she, Ed?'

'We were in competition for her, but Bert won out.'

'We had eleven wonderful years together,' said Bert, 'and when she went it was quick. She had a heart attack – a weakness no one knew about. I came home from work to find her dead in a chair. It looked like she'd just fallen asleep. Andrea was staying with her grandparents for a few days. It was half-term and she'd gone there because Phyllis was feeling a bit tired – under the weather.'

A silence settled over the room, broken only by the ticking of a grandfather clock Bert had said was once his father's.

After a minute or so, he cleared his throat. 'Anyway, you want to know about what's been going on at St Botolph's, don't you? You don't want to hear about me.'

'Yes, I do. Thank you for telling me about Phyllis.'

'Thank you for listening.'

I waited a few seconds, then continued, 'So, can you tell me what you saw and heard last night? I know that you've spoken to the police, but I'd be grateful if you could tell me everything you remember. Zillah's mother is out of her mind with worry about her daughter, and has asked me to look into what happened.'

'Well, as I told the police, some time after ten – I'm not sure exactly when – I heard raised voices and came out to take a look, in case it was someone up to no good. And there, in the graveyard, I saw Zillah, shouting at Hengist: I could tell it was him because I could see his eye patch, and she had something in her hand, though I couldn't make out what it was. She was shouting something like, "I trusted you". He kept telling her to be quiet, but she was having none of that. Then she sort of *ran* at him, and they both disappeared round the other side of the church.'

I was silent, thinking hard. Had Hengist drawn Zillah into a sexual relationship that had gone wrong? Evangeline was adamant that Zillah had been in a relationship with Laurie, the young man from Norwich. Could she have been involved with both of them?

At least I now knew she was alive and well, though I was no closer to finding out where she was staying.

'Hengist was found close to the church porch. Can you see that from your garden?'

''Fraid not. My garden looks out on the back of the churchyard. I'll show you.'

With some effort he pulled himself out of the chair and led us through double doors into a small garden bursting with dahlias and chrysanthemums. A wooden picket fence divided the garden from the back of the churchyard – an area that was less groomed and tidy than the section at the front of the church. However, the side-gate that led to the church hall was clearly visible, and the path that wound its way around untended graves. I took a couple of photos on my phone and we returned to the lounge.

'And did you see Zillah again?' I asked, once we were seated.

Bert shook his big, heavy head. 'No. She must have left through the main gate.'

'And did you hear anything else?'

Bert's big brow wrinkled. 'I think I heard someone crying, but that was later on, and by then I was in bed, half-asleep, so I didn't get up to take a look.'

I thanked Bert, and asked him to get in touch if he remembered anything else. Then, as we were about to leave, his daughter Andrea arrived. A tall woman with greying hair pulled back into a ponytail, she had an easy, capable way about her.

After we'd introduced ourselves, I asked her whether she'd seen anything unusual on the night Hengist was killed.

'Not really. I drop in on Dad most afternoons after work, and often stay for something to eat. I saw Hengist getting out of his car at about seven o'clock, and remembered thinking it was unusual for him to arrive so early. The actors turned up later. I cooked tea for me and Dad and left at about eight.'

'I've remembered something else,' said Bert 'Didn't we hear shouting while we were having our tea?'

Andrea frowned. 'Now you mention it, we did hear raised voices, but I assumed it was kids. In the evenings they hang around in the little park close to the churchyard and make a racket.'

I scribbled in my notebook, wondering why Hengist had arrived an hour before the rehearsal was due to start.

'And as I drove back through the village around twenty to eleven – I'd been in Wells, at the film club – I saw a woman I didn't know rushing out of the churchyard. She had short black hair in a bob, and was wearing some funny coat that was longer one side than the other.'

I only knew one woman who wore that sort of coat.

Mindy.

19

In which we see how members of the Peasmarsh Players react to the tragedy

Janette Tinker

Flopped on her bed, Janette let herself give way to tears. She'd kept herself together while she was working at the deli, making coffees, serving yummy brownies and sandwiches, smiling at the customers, but at the end of her afternoon shift, she'd come home with an overwhelming feeling of disappointment weighing her down.

Oh, she understood that the acting profession was not a barrel of laughs, that you had to be resilient and take the knocks, but this had been her *big chance* – her passport to getting an agent, moving to London, finding professional work. She deserved it, after what she'd done to make sure Hengist got his agent friend to come to see her.

It just wasn't fair.

And as well as being bitterly disappointed, she was shivery from shock. She couldn't believe it. Why would anyone do that? Yes, Hengist was a total tosser who thought the world revolved around him, but he was a good director, and he *got things done.* In that respect he was like her: they were two of a kind. She hadn't liked him, but she'd admired his drive and energy.

And now he was dead, and her acting career was down the toilet.

She heard a tap on the door, and her mother calling from the other side. 'Can I come in? I've made you a cup of tea.'

Janette dragged herself into a sitting position, so she was leaning against the pillows. 'Of course.'

Her mum appeared, carrying a small tray with two mugs of tea and a plate of chocolate biscuits. 'Here you are, treasure. Have a cuppa: it always makes things better.'

'Thanks,' she croaked.

'It's not the end of the world, you know,' said her mum, patting her leg. 'It's just a little setback. We've had those before, haven't we? What about the time the bus broke down on the way to Norwich and you missed your chance to audition for *Joseph and the Amazing Technicolour Dreamcoat*?'

Janette managed a watery smile. 'I made a right fuss, didn't I? I sulked for about three days after that.'

'You were disappointed, that's all. And it was probably a naff old production.'

'Do you think so?' said Janette, knowing this wasn't true but appreciating her mum's efforts to cheer her up.

'Oh, yes. I heard it was pants. Big girl's pants.'

This made Janette giggle so hard she spluttered into her tea.

'Anyway, I've been thinking. I've got a little bit saved up, and so have you. Why don't you make an appointment with that agent Hengist told you about? You could combine it with an open casting session.'

A flicker of hope lit up in Janette's chest. 'Do you think she'd see me?'

'I don't see why not. And we've got those head-shots, haven't we?'

Feeling tears threaten again, Janette jumped off the bed and threw her arms round her mum. 'Thanks, Mum. I love you so much. You know that, don't you?'

'And I love you, sweetheart.'

Her mum had been looking online and had found some open casting sessions on *The Stage*'s website.

'Look: there's one for *Sweeney Todd* tomorrow. Do you fancy a little trip to London? The care home have agreed I can have a couple of days off.'

Janette felt the big grey cloud hanging over her head evaporating. 'Oh, I'd love to play Sweeney Todd's daughter! And I've learned some of the songs from the show with my singing teacher.'

'There we are, then.'

Excited, they chatted a bit more before her mum left to do her evening shift. Janette dug out the sheet music for *Sweeney Todd* and started running through the songs. Then the Deli rang and asked if she could do a few extra hours at a big party that evening, adding, 'We'd need you to come in as soon as possible, if you can, to help set out the food and drink.'

Janette took that as a good omen, put on some eye make-up and hurried out of the house, pausing only to ring Jem, who was still down in Sussex. He didn't pick up – not unusual when he was working – so she left a message telling him about her plans, and hinting that they'd be able to snatch a couple of hours in bed when they were both back in Wells.

He'd been a bit down in the dumps lately, and that would cheer him up.

* *

Iain Bright

In his untidy, fusty bedroom – a room distinctly out of kilter with the rest of the immaculate Bright family home, Iain opened up his laptop for the tenth time that day. There was something he needed to check. His eyes scanned the screen as he scrolled through the pages.

He let out a little yelp then slammed the lid shut.

Fingers trembling, he extracted a cigarette from the packet he'd hidden in his drawer and went over to the window to smoke. Perched half on the sill he looked down over the garden his mother, Mindy, had created over the last couple of years, since they moved here. It was orderly, immaculate, designed by a posh pal of hers from London, featuring a semi-circular pond, several ugly metal sculptures and beds crammed full of spiky green plants. The only part of the garden Iain liked was the woodland grove at the back, where Mindy had shipped in a few fully-grown trees (when she wanted something, she wanted it *now* and not in a few years' time) and scattered wildflower seeds on the ground.

As he sucked on his cigarette the nicotine calmed his fevered brain. He'd have to talk to his mother – explain the deal he'd made with Dad. Persuade her that she had to honour Hengist's promise.

The police must have thought he was a hard-hearted bastard for not bursting into tears when they arrived this morning to tell him his father was dead.

Well he *was* sorry his dad was dead, but he wasn't pole-axed by grief. There was something mean and cruel about Hengist. He'd made Iain's life a misery for as long as he could remember, telling him he was a lazy bones, a drifter, because all he wanted to do when he hit his teens was smoke dope and read books. He'd made him take part in his tin-pot plays – something Iain would have quite enjoyed, because he knew he was good at it, if Hengist hadn't patronised him and controlled his every move. And Hengist had been on his case for years to get a girlfriend, saying it wasn't normal for a boy of his age to be holed up in his room all the time.

Of course, Hengist didn't know what Iain was getting up to in there. Even Hengist couldn't stop him locking the door so he could get on with things in private.

The joke was, he wasn't even sure Hengist was his father. One evening when he was fourteen and they were all on holiday in Crete, his mother had necked too many strong gin and tonics, and told him in a slurred voice that Hengist might not be his dad. 'After all, you're nothing like him. You don't have his drive or his energy. When I first met Hengist I was involved with another man – a hopeless case but so sweet-natured. So gentle. Not like *him*.' She'd spoken loud enough that Hengist, who was moving in on the lush waitress, could hear every word.

There was no more flirting with gorgeous Greek girls from Hengist that holiday, and no more confessions from his mother. To this day, Iain didn't know whether she'd made it all up to be spiteful.

Anyway, the old man was gone.

And he was way up the creek without a paddle.

* *

Cedric Williams

Cedric Williams was basking in happiness as he searched for flights and planned his itinerary. From Nice he'd go to Saint Tropez to soak up the ambience of the town where Paul Signac, one of the leaders of the pointillist movement, built his studio and lived for much of his life. As he clicked and scrolled, he could almost feel the warmth of the sunny French Riviera, where he could research his book in the morning, snooze in the afternoons, and sip fragrant wine in the evenings.

Now he wasn't tied to a three-month rehearsal schedule for *Jeeves Pulls it Off*, a huge cloud of worry had shifted from over his head. He felt as if a prison door had finally been opened, and the whole world beckoned.

When he'd heard that Hengist was dead he'd been so shocked he had to sit down for a few minutes. And he found himself shedding a few tears because though Hengist was a dominant bastard, Cedric had admired his drive and his talent, and being bashed on the head with a chunk of gravestone is a grim way to go.

Over dinner he'd explain to Sheila that he needed to head to St Tropez as soon as possible to do some essential research. He'd pretended that his publisher was pressing him to finish the book – which was almost true – and she'd patted him on the leg, as she always did, saying, 'Sounds like a good plan, darling.'

Downstairs he could hear her singing through the chorus of *Carmen* as she prepared their evening meal of lasagne; she had an excellent voice (of course) and was a leading light in the local operatic society. In fact there were few things she couldn't do.

Except make him love her.

20

In which Rags turns to her dad for advice

I was ravenous when I got in, and devoured a plate of bread, cheese and pickles while thinking over my meeting with Bert. There seemed to be no doubt that Zillah had been at St Botolph's and had threatened Hengist, but I wasn't convinced that she'd killed him. Remembering the old dictum that murders are most often committed by family members, I decided I needed to pay a visit to his nearest and dearest.

Had Mindy been at the churchyard that evening? And who was the person Bert heard crying?

I rang the offices of the local rag, leaving a message asking whether they'd accept an extended obituary/feature about Hengist Bright, 'a much loved local theatre director.' Since I offered to do this for nothing, and added that I'd been at the rehearsal on the night he died, I expected them to say yes. That would give me my cover to go and question his family, friends (if I could find any) and the Peasmarsh Players.

Then I rang my old pal from the Met – Paddy McKee, of the ginger beard and magic computer skills. Though now retired from the police force, he could lay his hands on all sorts of information, usually for the princely sum of £100. He'd always had a soft spot for me, and produced the goods within a day or so.

But I was dismayed to get through to a message on his mobile saying he was in the USA for a few days, and wouldn't be answering calls until he returned to his office. I left a message saying I wanted the lowdown on Hengist Bright – any criminal convictions or brushes with the police, any debts, any links with someone who might want to do him in.

Feeling restless, I rang Dad. He answered in the anxious voice he'd used since Gwendolyn reappeared. 'What is it? Has something happened? Is she causing trouble?'

'It's nothing to do with Mum,' I said, feeling angry with her all over again for destroying his peace of mind. 'I hardly see her. I just wanted to bring you up to date on things, and get your advice.'

'Right-o then. Fire away,' he said, sounding calmer already.

I explained that Julian had asked me to look into Hengist's death, since Zillah seemed to be the prime suspect, but neither she nor I believed she'd killed him. 'But I wondered whether he'd got any enemies in the Players – anyone who might hold a massive grudge against him – apart from Alfie, of course, who was livid about not getting the part of Bertie Wooster.'

'Well he wasn't everyone's cup of tea. He put people's backs up. But I can't think of anyone who hated him enough to kill him. Tell you what: I'll have a word with Susie and get back to you. She's been involved with the Players for much longer than I have.'

'Thanks, Dad. That would be great.'

After I'd hung up I poured myself a large glass of Merlot and turned on the TV. Now I was connected to broadband I could catch up with all the twaddle I'd missed. I spent a happy half hour watching an old episode of *Come Dine with Me* before Dad rang back.

'I don't know if this is significant, but Susie says that Hengist had some sort of falling-out with Cedric at the after-show party for *All Our Sons*. They'd always been friends, but since then the air between them has been decidedly frosty.'

'But he cast him as Jeeves.'

'I know.'

'Come to think of it, Cedric did seem rather tense when we measured him up for his costume.'

'And that's unlike him. Susie says until recently he's been relaxed, chatty – more than happy to take the lead parts.'

I thought for a moment. 'Do you think Hengist has been hitting on his wife? He has a reputation for that sort of thing.'

'Hmmm. I've met Sheila, and I doubt that she's his type.' He paused. 'There have been rumours about Hengist and Janette, but I never believed them. She's devoted to that boyfriend of hers.'

And Jem was devoted to her – perhaps *too* devoted.

I went to bed soon after that. Half-awake, I heard Gwendolyn come in and get herself a glass of water from the kitchen. I still didn't know where she was going or what she was up to, but I was grateful for her absences, and had too much on my plate right now to give them much thought.

21

In which Rags sets to work

At nine-thirty the next morning I got a call from the *Fakenham and Wells Times*. Yes, they'd be delighted for me to write a feature on Hengist Bright – an obituary but also an account of what had happened on the night he died, though they were unfortunately unable to pay me. No surprise there but at least I had a cover for asking questions if needed.

I decided to head over to Hengist's house that morning. So that I was prepared, I ran some searches on Hengist Bright, and discovered that he'd been directing productions in Norfolk for the past decade or so, and had been interviewed by the local press a few times. Reviews of his productions were uniformly good, though the reviewer poked fun at the last production (*All my Sons*), pointing out that one of the lead characters forgot he was meant to be on stage in the final act, and had to be extracted from his dressing room. Poor Alfie: he'd never live that down.

Then I ran a few searches on Mindy Bright, and came

up with precisely nothing. She wasn't on social media, and I concluded that her professional life was conducted under her maiden name.

I decided to have a catch-up with Toots before I set off; she might be able to tell me more about Hengist's life and the state of his marriage. Toots was delighted to hear from me, and invited me round for coffee and croissants – an invitation I happily accepted.

While she brewed up some coffee I sat at her kitchen table swooning at the sight of the pink roses growing in profusion outside her window. It almost made me wish I had a garden. As soon as we were seated with our breakfast, I asked Toots whether she knew if Hengist had any enemies. Her answer was similar to the ones others had given: though not popular, he'd been admired and appreciated.

'The Peasmarsh Players have gone from strength to strength since he got involved. He's chosen great scripts and directed excellent productions.'

'And what about his marriage to Mindy? Would you say they were happy together?'

She thought for a moment. 'Mindy plays her cards close to her chest: it's hard to know what she thinks and feels about anything. But I do know that she was crazy about Hengist.'

'And their son, Iain? How did he get on with his father?'

'Badly. Hengist was cold and controlling; I seldom saw him show affection towards his son.'

'That's sad.'

'Apparently their relationship was much better when Iain was younger. Evangeline has told me that the family used to visit Wells before they moved up here permanently, and the three of them went crabbing together, and took the little train to the beach – that sort of thing. She says they looked happy enough.'

'So their differences could be just down to normal teenage troubles?'

Toots shook her head. 'It seemed worse than that to me, but then I don't have children, so am no expert.'

As I finished up the last of my croissant I remembered I had something else to ask Toots. 'I can't find Mindy Bright anywhere on social media. Do you know what name she uses for her consultancy work?'

'Someone once told me her real name's Amanda, but I've no idea of her surname.'

'Well, thanks for breakfast. I'd better get on my way.'

Toots sighed. 'Before you go, there's something else you should know.'

'Yes?'

'On the night Hengist died, as I was getting ready for bed, I heard a racket outside my window. Someone had shoved over a bin: it happens now and then when people who are a bit the worse for wear take a short-cut through my street. There's a small path runs round the back of my garden, which only locals know about.'

She came to a halt. I waited.

'And when I looked out, I saw a young man weaving around, with what looked like blood on his clothes.' She took another breath. 'Though I didn't get a clear look at his face, I think it was Jem.'

Jem's name was on The Peasmarsh Players contact list. I rang him as soon as I was back in my flat. He didn't pick up, so I left a message asking him if we could meet up, as I wanted a few shelves putting up in the flat.

Then I made a list of people who'd been at the rehearsal. I needed to ring them all.

Janette Tinker
Cedric Williams
Iain Bright
Betzy Stretch
Dave Bennett

Janette picked up after the first ring, sounding remarkably cheerful. All was explained when she told me that she and her mum were on their way to London.

'We're going to an open casting session for *Sweeney Todd* today, and the agent has agreed to see me tomorrow.'

'That's brilliant! I'm writing a piece about Hengist for the local press, and they want some information about his work with The Players. Did Tuesday's rehearsal go as normal after Toots and I left?'

'Yes. As far as I can remember. We worked for a bit on the first scene, and finished just before ten.'

'So what time did you leave?'

'Straightaway. I'd done a long shift in the deli, so I was knackered.'

'Did you get a lift back?'

'No. I walked home. Sometimes Jem picks me up, but he's doing a big carpentry job with a mate's firm down in Sussex for a few days.'

'When did he go?'

'Monday.'

So Toots couldn't have seen him weaving around with blood on his shirt.

Next I tried Cedric Williams, only to find that his mobile was switched off. When I rang his landline, his wife picked up.

'Double three, double two, eight six.'

I explained that I was hoping to have a word with Cedric, and she went into gales of laughter, as if I'd told a hilarious joke. 'You won't have any luck getting hold of him. He's on his way to France to do some research on his next book, and when he does that he always switches off his phone. Says it stops him being distracted.'

'Then could you perhaps let me know what time he got home on Tuesday night?'

'Well, he was tucked up in bed when I got in from playing bridge at around 11. He suffers from migraines, poor lamb, so he was holed up in the spare room.'

So Cedric could have stayed behind after the rehearsal, or returned later.

When I called Betzy Stretch, she said, in a dry voice, that she'd rather talk to me in person and would telephone when she had some spare time.

Iain Bright's mobile was switched off.

Dave Bennett picked up within a couple of rings. When I asked him what time he left the rehearsal he told me that Iain had given him a lift back to Wells, adding: 'We went for a drink in The Fleece.' He paused. 'I can't believe Hengist has gone – there was something so vital and alive about him'

'I know what you mean.'

He asked me how I was getting on in Wells, and we chatted for a few minutes. Then, just before I hung up he said, 'Can I ask you something?'

'Of course.'

'Can I take you for a drink this evening?'

22

In which Rags visits the house of the deceased

The Bright family home was situated between Holkham and Burnham Market. Under a sky thickening with bruise coloured clouds I drove along the coast road then turned left into the small side road Toots had told me to look out for. A few hundred metres up the road I came across an elegant but characterless modern house. I left my car on the roadside verge, and opened a spanking new five-bar gate. The front of the house boasted a large gravel drive, on which an old VW was parked – Iain's, I presumed.

I rang the door bell. A volley of dog barks exploded from inside the house but no one answered the door. I looked up and saw an open window, and caught a whiff of cigarette smoke. I rang the door bell again. This time I heard footsteps coming down the stairs and across the hall before the door was yanked open.

The drawn face of Iain Bright appeared. 'Yes?'

'It's Rags Whistledown,' I said, showing him my NUJ card. 'I've been asked to write a feature on your father's life and work for the local press. Could we please have a word?'

'My mother's not in. She's on her way back from Budapest.'

'I'd love to get a rounded picture of your father and your thoughts would be valuable,' I said, watching his tight, unhappy face.

'Look: I don't have time to talk to you.'

'I can offer you some expenses,' I said, as he started to close the door. Surprise flashed across his face, making him look younger and more vulnerable. 'How much?'

'Fifty pounds. Possibly more if I talk to you again.'

He pulled the door open. 'I suppose you'd better come in then.'

I followed him across the large, parquet-tiled hall to a sterile living room furnished with two huge cream leather sofas, an artsy rug and a discreet television. Half a dozen minimalist black and white prints that probably cost a bomb hung on the walls.

High-pitched dog barks rose intermittently from an adjacent room. Iain pulled a face. 'That's Beckett. He's a pain in the arse. Ignore him: he'll shut up in a bit.'

I winced inwardly: the way he behaved to the dog was probably the way he'd been treated by Hengist. He flopped down on one of the sofas, sprawling out so that I couldn't sit beside him. Though he had Hengist's elegant features he had an unkempt, unloved look about him. His jeans were grubby, his tee-shirt frayed. I'd smelled cigarette smoke on him when he opened the door, mingled with stale sweat.

I perched on the other sofa and got out my notebook.

'So: tell me about your father. What was notable or extraordinary about him?'

Iain yawned, chewing over my question. When he spoke, his voice was quiet and dry. 'He was talented and driven – a fine director. And he was a stickler for detail.

Everything had to be just right. He had – how can I put it? – high standards.'

'How long had he been working with The Peasmarsh Players?'

'About nine years. We lived in London for a while then moved to Norfolk when I was twelve. He'd always wanted to run a theatre company, and The Peasmarsh Players were looking for someone.'

'So he ran the theatre group as well as directing the plays?'

'He and my mother ran it together: he was the chair, and she was the vice-chair. She's an ace at admin, and he handles all the creative stuff. They're voted in every year by the committee.' He gave a melancholy shrug. 'The Players could replace them with other people, but why would they?'

'And I gather that you acted in some of the plays when you were younger.'

His shoulders moved closer to his ears. 'Well – yes. But I stopped when I went into the sixth form.'

'And what sort of a father was he?'

Iain blinked. 'Pardon?'

'It's clear he was a talented director,' I said, with a gentle smile to encourage him to speak, 'but I'd love to get a sense of how he was at home, with his family.'

I could hear Iain's breathing, as he struggled to respond to this question. Then he gathered himself together and forged on. 'Busy. Always busy. He used to teach drama at some tin-pot community college, but as soon as Mum started making big money he gave that up. All he really cared about was directing. It consumed him.'

'And what was your relationship with him?' I said softly.

The sound of his harsh breathing filled the room. Then he jumped up from the sofa muttering, 'I'm sorry. I can't go on with this,' and made a run for it. I heard footsteps thudding up the stairs and the slam of a door.

I sat there feeling like a heel. I probably should have waited until Mindy was home. Yes, he was twenty-one and legally an adult, but he was clearly vulnerable. After a few minutes I went up the stairs. Two of the doors leading off the landing were shut. I tapped tentatively on one of them and opened it to find a palatial bathroom. When I tapped on the second door, a broken voice called, 'Go away.'

'I'm sorry,' I said. 'Please let me in. I just want to know you're all right.'

'Go away!' he yelled.

'OK.' I dug into my bag. 'Look, at least let me give you the money I promised.'

That got him to open the door. Looking about twelve years old, with a red, tear-stained face, he grabbed the notes and stuffed them into a pocket of his jeans. 'Do you want to know the truth about my father? The only thing he was interested in was *himself*. He didn't give a fuck about me, or anyone else for that matter. And I'd like you to go now.'

With that, he shut the door in my face.

I drove away feeling furious. I knew Hengist Bright was a narcissist, but to be cruel to your own child is unforgiveable, in my book. After years of emotional neglect, Iain was clearly angry with his father – angry enough to kill him? Dave had said that they left at 10 and had a drink in Wells, but Iain could easily have driven back to the church to have it out with his father.

And then there was the question of Mindy. Iain believed she'd been in Budapest last night, but Andrea had seen her – or someone very like her – in Peasmarsh around 10.30 pm.

One thing was crystal clear: Iain urgently needed money.

Then it came to me: I knew why he'd agreed to play Bertie Wooster.

Hengist must have offered to pay him for his services.

When I got home I went on to my laptop and checked the status of flights to and from Budapest on the night Hengist was killed.

After a bit of digging I discovered that the flight scheduled to depart at 11 pm from Stansted had been cancelled due to a technical fault, and the passengers transferred to other flights leaving early the following morning.

Mindy had some explaining to do when she returned.

23

In which we find a few answers and uncover more questions

Evangeline Nielsen

Evangeline Nielsen hummed as she finished drying the glasses and plates from the night before. Holding one up to the light, she absorbed the beauty of the rainbow prism created by the shaft of sun streaming through it.

Quiet footsteps came up behind her. Arms crept round her waist, and a male body pushed up against her. Mmm. She arched her spine so that her body pressed against his in return.

'Shall we go upstairs?'

Wordless, she followed, unzipping her skirt as she went.

She knew that people thought she was an uptight old bag, but they didn't know about this secret life of hers – a precious life of sexual satisfaction. When she was thirteen she found that if she sat on a certain seat on the school bus she was able to bring herself to orgasm without anyone knowing it was happening. The change in her breathing was never noticed in the noisy chaos that was the upper deck, with things being thrown around and voices yelling jokes, gossip, insults. This skill had always been her secret treasure.

And now she had someone to share it with.

Half an hour later she was downstairs again, tidying away the glasses, turning the key on the corner cabinet that sat in her lounge, then slipping the key into a hidden pocket in her bag.

Best to be safe not sorry.

* *

Mindy Bright

Mindy knew she was driving too slowly down the A1065. Cars kept overtaking, with the drivers giving her filthy looks.

The truth was, she didn't want to face the house without Hengist. Didn't want to arrange his funeral. Didn't want to sort out his will.

Didn't want to talk to the police.

A lance of pain pierced her chest. With a gasp, she squealed to a halt in a parking place beneath the shade of some pine trees. As soon as she stopped the car, tears leapt from her eyes and poured down her cheeks.

'Oh!'

Pulling a clutch of tissues from her handbag, she mopped up the flood until the flow dried to a dribble and finally stopped, leaving her with bloodshot, itchy eyes.

At least she no longer felt like something was crouching in her chest and threatening to explode. She fished out a make-up bag and repaired her face, using the rear-view mirror of the Mercedes convertible she'd left at Stansted for the past couple of nights. Then, once her breathing had settled, she pulled out on to the road again.

She'd got the message that Hengist was dead on her first morning in Hungary. Her colleagues had tried to persuade her to turn round and go home immediately, but she'd refused, for reasons she didn't quite understand. All she knew was that she needed to stabilise herself by performing as impeccably as always in the work arena. She'd lied and said that she wasn't able to get a flight on the first day, but in fact she'd needed those hours to steady herself for what was ahead.

It wasn't until she reached the airport to fly home that she started to wobble – literally. As she joined the queue for security she felt the floor shift beneath her feet. Gritting her teeth, she willed the ground to settle until she could walk without staggering and lurching. Then she sat like a zombie in the departure lounge, watching the planes taxi to and fro.

She walled up her grief and sorrow during the flight to Stansted: she was damned if she was going to sob and howl in front of a plane full of inane tourists, half of whom were stinking of booze after a stag do. She kept herself busy doing advanced Sudoku and cryptic crosswords: she'd always found that keeping her brain occupied was a necessary distraction from whatever Hengist was getting up to.

For she knew about his infidelities – the major ones. Throughout their marriage she'd pretended they didn't really matter, and he'd always been so contrite afterwards – so attentive that they often ended up in bed.

But an early menopause had put an end to their passionate making-up sessions. It had shrunk her sexual desire from a river to a puddle, and made Hengist's behaviour unbearable. Surely it was the cruellest joke biology played on the female of the species – much worse than periods and PMT. Hot sweats, dry skin, minimal sex drive – she'd suffered them all. She took HRT, prescribed by an expensive Harley Street doctor, but that only mitigated her symptoms, and didn't remove them.

Or perhaps she'd just become weary of coping with his rampant screwing around. She'd got fed up with forgiveness. After a recent episode with the daughter of a good friend, she'd warned him that if he transgressed again she wouldn't stand for it.

He'd sworn that he'd reformed. 'I promise, my darling. It will never, ever happen again.'

Some promise!

This latest outrage had been more than she could stand. It was so *humiliating*.

Drastic action had been called for.

* *

Jem Townley

Though Jem Townley could have done with a day off, he'd come to do this job because he wanted to earn as much as he could so he could put his plan into action.

The afternoon was warm. Sparrows were clustering in the blanket of ivy creeping up the wall of what had once been a hay barn, and now housed three Blue Sky Cottages holiday lets.

He mopped his face with a cotton rag. He was trying to hang a door in one of the properties, and the bastard thing wouldn't fit the frame. He'd have to take it down again and plane a millimetre or two off the bottom and the side. It was always like this at Blue Sky Cottages: Alfie wanted him to take off a perfectly good door and replace it with one that had been dipped in acid to remove all the paint, stripping the wood of its natural oils, and encouraging splits and cracks. The sort of customers they got here liked this sort of crap. He'd caught them sniggering, whispering that he was 'Normal for Norfolk' after they heard his accent. The women eyed him up, though – their gaze lingering on his tool belt, his biceps, as if they'd like to eat him for breakfast.

No chance. He had his Janette – his beautiful girl, who gave him a fuzzy feeling that filled his chest whenever he saw her. Yes, they had sex – pretty good sex – whenever they had her house or his to themselves. But it wasn't that. In fact he'd had better sex with his first girlfriend, who was plump and spotty but who'd stared into his eyes and begged him to do it harder, deeper. But once they were out of the sack they'd had nothing in common. She'd wittered on about her hair, her friends, her mum. He'd sat there bored to tears, wishing she'd stop biting her nails.

With Janette it was different. They always had plenty to talk about. Admittedly, it was usually about her – her ambitions and plans for the future – but she'd always listen to his grumbles if there was something he needed to get off his chest. And when he did a good joinery job, like making that bespoke table for the Deli, she celebrated with him, and told him how bloody amazing he was.

With a grunt, he freed the door from its hinges and carried it to the work bench on the patio outside the property's front door. He laid it down, picked up the plane that had been his grandfather's before him, and started to shave off the excess wood, using a spirit level now and then to check that he was creating a straight edge to the door.

As he worked, the events of the past ten days churned round in his head. He wished he wasn't such a hothead. But when Janette came back from London she'd be full of news about the casting call and the agent that prick Hengist had dangled in front of her nose. Surely she'd have forgotten about him turning up late that night. And even if she did bring it up he'd say he'd been getting ready for an early start the next day and had lost track of the time.

Then he'd get her talking about her plans to move to London, and though he'd be gutted to leave Wells – his family had lived here for three generations – he'd suggest they move as soon as they could.

Satisfied that he'd planed smooth, straight edges, he straightened up and mopped the sweat off his face again.

Yes: that was the answer. It would be best to get out of Wells as soon as possible.

Before anyone found out what he had done.

* *

Alfie Adams

Pacing to and fro, heart beating fast, Alfie watched Jem pick up the door as if it weighed next to nothing.

Lucky Jem. He had nothing to worry about. He hadn't received a visit from the police first thing in the morning. He hadn't been sat down and questioned as if he were a criminal, just because of something he'd said in the pub. Everyone said things like, 'I could kill him' didn't they? He'd explained that to the police officer – an uptight blonde female who resembled one the Hitchcock's heroines he adored, but without the glamour. This woman – DI Cooper – had looked at him with icy green eyes and asked him to account for his movements on the night Hengist was killed, adding, 'We know you were in the Edinburgh pub earlier in the evening.'

He'd blustered and said he'd met up with friends in another pub after he left the Eddie. But when she asked him for names, he'd stuttered that he'd forgotten because he'd had far too much to drink that night.

'And of course, I walked home,' he added, seeing her eyes narrow as she wrote down yet more in her little black book.

'Well perhaps you could contact the incident room when you've remembered who you were with,' she'd said, adding, 'so that we can eliminate you from our enquiries.'

Thank heavens, she'd gone after that, taking with her the

chubby police officer who was her sidekick. Now he'd have to dredge up some tame acquaintance from his school days, and slip him a few quid to swear they spent the latter part of the evening together.

Ma wasn't here – she'd gone to visit an aged aunt in Worthing – and for the first time in years Alfie found himself missing her, longing for her return. Yes, Ma was a pain in the arse, but she'd know how to get him out of this mess: she'd been doing it since he was almost expelled from school. Perhaps he could persuade her to swear that he'd gone straight back home after he'd got pissed in the Eddie.

In the mean time ... Alfie yanked the desk drawer open and extracted a wrap of white powder. Laid it out on his desk and took a couple of deep snorts of amphetamine through his silver straw. His nerves tingled, hummed as the chemicals dissolved at the back of his nose.

Ah. That was better.

24

***In which Rags is told that a person
can live off water and fresh air***

After I left Hengist's house, I drove back to Wells and took
a walk along the East Quay. I wanted to get my thoughts in
order, and walking helps me do that.

I needed to know if anyone else had shown up at the
church once the rehearsal was over.

Was Alfie there? Was he the person Bert heard 'crying'
later in the evening? When I saw him in the pub he was
certainly drunk enough to rage and weep.

Janette had told me that Jem was in Sussex on the night
of the murder, but Toots thought she might have seen him
in Wells that night.

As for Janette, I still thought it highly unlikely that
she was the murderer. Would she jeopardise her chances
of finding an agent by attacking Hengist, even if he was
demanding sexual favours? I just couldn't see it.

Mindy's flight had been cancelled, and it seemed likely
she was the woman Andrea had seen that night in the
churchyard.

And to my list of possible suspects, I needed to add Iain Bright. He hated his father, and had probably been bribed to appear in the production. His mental state was volatile, to say the least. I couldn't see him as a calculating killer, but could he have returned to St Botolph's, argued with Hengist and then killed him in a fit of rage?

That left Dave and Betzy. Neither of them appeared to have a motive, but where Hengist was concerned anything was possible. Dave could have returned to the church after he and Iain shared their pint, though I could see no reason why he'd want to harm Hengist. And Betzy didn't have an alibi that I knew of, though I was still waiting to talk to her.

I decided I'd have a bite to eat before starting my phone calls, but as I climbed the stairs I could hear music coming from the flat. Oh, crap. That meant Gwendolyn was back. Approaching the flat door, I realised that it was *All I Want*, the first song on *Blue*, my favourite Joni Mitchell album. The song's irrepressible hope had appealed to me twenty years ago, but as I got older I found myself drawn to the more melancholy, intense songs such as *A Case of You*. Gwendolyn must have found the CD and was playing it on the machine that lived in the kitchen.

When I came in the flat door, she was singing along and dancing in the lounge, hands lifted above her head, hips swaying to the beat. Catching sight of me, she threw me a beatific glance and beckoned to me to come and join her in the dance.

'No thanks. I've got too much to do,' I snapped, sounding like a repressive school marm.

'Come *on*! Don't be an old misery. Just go with the flow.'

'No, really, I ...'

But she'd grabbed hold of my hands and was drawing

me into the centre of the room where she'd shoved back the coffee table to make some space. Reluctant but unable to resist I started to move to the rhythm of Joni's optimistic lines, wrapped in the scent of patchouli and warm skin. As Gwendolyn danced, her hair flew out behind her like pale-gold silk, her eyes met mine, and her lips opened into a radiant smile.

Something opened up in my heart: I remembered why it was that people fell in love with her. I'd been in love with her myself when I was a small child and we'd caught the bus to Hunstanton to amble along the beach and through the dunes. As we walked, she'd bent down to tell me the names of flowers: *sea thistle, cornflower, scarlet pimpernel, shepherd's purse*. I'd been captivated, entranced by the words, by her perfume and the soft sweep of her hair, sure that no one had a mother as beautiful as mine.

The song ended and she bounced into the kitchen to play it again. It was then that I noticed a small, open suitcase beside the sofa. Inside, clothes were neatly folded beside a couple of books and a packet of incense sticks.

'Going somewhere?' I asked, over the music.

'Just for a few days.'

'Anywhere nice?'

'Divine!' She giggled. 'Though you wouldn't understand. You're too earth-bound.'

So we were back to that broken record. Refusing to be drawn, I went into the kitchen and turned down the music. 'When will you be back?'

She stopped dancing and put her hands on her hips. 'Do you know what? You sound just like my mother. I never questioned you like this, did I? I gave you the freedom to do whatever you wanted.'

It was on the tip of my tongue to say that she'd never been interested in me or where I was going after Tarquin, my step brother, was born, but I turned away and switched on the kettle. I didn't have time for her taunts and riddles right now.

'Well, whatever you're doing, I hope you have a fantastic time,' I called, over my shoulder.

She bounced up behind me and stopped the CD. 'Don't you worry: I will,' she whispered, her breath hot in my ear.

'Would you like a slice of toast?'

She laughed, but it wasn't a pleasant sound. There was a touch of the cackle about it. 'No thank you.'

'Or a cup of coffee?'

'I have no need of earthly nourishment. Not any more.'

I turned to look at her, and realised her eyes were burning and her face bright – too bright. 'Are you all right?'

'Better than all right. I'm flying!'

I looked her up and down: she was skinnier than when she first arrived. 'Have you been eating properly?' I asked, fighting off a pang of guilt, because I hadn't been paying much attention to shopping or to meals.

'Listen to you!' she squawked. Then, moving closer, 'I don't *need* to eat. All I need is air and water.'

A shiver chased up the back of my neck. 'That's crazy. Of course you need to eat.'

'Don't tell me what to do! I'm your mother.'

'Then start acting like one.'

'Oh, here we go again.' Her voice took on a mocking tone. 'Poor little Ragnell ...'

'Don't ...'

'... always whining and complaining because Mummy's not at her beck and call.'

'Shut up!' I yelled, as rage boiled over in my chest. 'And if that's how you feel about me you can bugger off.'

She narrowed her eyes. 'I'll pick up the rest of my luggage after the retreat.'

And with that, she zipped up the little case, picked it up and ran down the stairs.

I stood there, winded. What the heck had happened there? Why did conversations with Gwendolyn always turn into blazing rows? With dismay I felt my eyes filling with tears. Yes, I felt five years old again, wanting love, wanting affection, but needing to dance attendance on her to get it.

My phone rang. I grabbed at it, hoping against all logic that she'd rung to apologise.

Instead a soft Norfolk voice said, 'Rags? It's Andrea here. You said to ring if I thought of anything.'

I struggled to bring my brain back into focus. 'Yes?' I said, trying to place her.

'Bert's daughter. We met yesterday.'

'Oh, yes. Sorry – I was in the middle of something.'

'Only I've remembered that there's been a van parked up near St Botolph's a couple of times in the past week, and I think I saw it when I was driving home on the night Mr Bright was killed. It had a picture on the side – a hammer, I think – and a name. I can't remember the full name, but it was something like Tom, or John. I think the surname began with a T.'

Jem Townley.

Jem had been there on the night Hengist was murdered.

25

In which Rags follows up an important lead

Right. Number one priority was to talk to Jem. He had motive and opportunity. It would only take about three hours to drive from Sussex to Norfolk when the roads were quiet. Easy enough to attack Hengist then drive back and be in bed by two.

I rang his number. This time he answered.

'Jem Townley here.'

I asked him if he'd come round to quote for putting up some shelves.

'I'm just finishing up a job but I could drop by in half an hour.'

The Jem who arrived was different to the one I'd met in the pub, full of beer, drooling over Janette. He was smartly dressed in worn but clean jeans and a white tee-shirt that showed off his muscular arms. The rich smell of sawdust clung to him, accompanied by the background scent of good soap. When I showed him where I wanted the shelves in the living room, he measured up, jotted down some neat figures in a black Moleskine notebook, adding a precise sketch where there were some old pipes to be accommodated. Taking out his phone, he inputted the figures and an estimate of labour hours, deducted twenty per cent then gave me an estimate of £240, including materials.

I said I'd have to think about it, as I was waiting for some money to come through, and offered him a cup of tea and a piece of cake.

After a brief hesitation, he accepted. I went into the kitchen to make the tea and cut two juicy slices of cherry cake bought from Fakenham market. As I watched him sink down on the sofa I could see that his good-natured face held a trace of sadness.

'Dreadful news about Hengist, isn't it?' I said, bringing in the tray and putting it on the coffee table in front of him.

'Yes.'

'I was there that night, and everything seemed to be as normal. I just can't imagine who would do a thing like that.'

'Neither can I,' said Jem, concentrating on his slice of cake.

'But I gather he wasn't that popular,' I continued, in gossipy mode. 'You knew him much better than me: can you think of anyone who was his enemy?'

'No.'

'Janette must be devastated. I know how much she was looking forward to being in the play.'

He shot me a sharp glance. 'You'd have to talk to her about that.'

Seeing I wasn't going to get anywhere with this, I changed the subject. 'Janette tells me you've been working in Sussex. I've got friends who've just been on holiday down there. They say it's gorgeous but very expensive.'

'You're telling me. It's even worse than Norfolk.'

'She said they stayed in an AirBnB and it cost £100 a night! Can you believe it?'

'Some people have got more money than sense.'

'Any recommendations of places to stay?'

'Nah. I always make my own arrangements.' He drained his mug and popped the last mouthful of cake into his mouth before standing up. 'I'd better be off. Get back to me if you want me to put up that shelving for you.'

'I will. And thanks for the discount.'

I said goodbye and watched him head off down the street. Then I dialled Toots' number.

She answered straightaway. After a few pleasantries I asked her about Jem's van. 'Could he sleep in there?'

She thought for a moment. 'Yes, I'm sure he could. Come to think of it, Janette once told me that they sometimes camp out in the van when she and Jem go away for a night or two.'

That settled it then. If Jem was sleeping in his van it would have been easy for him to drive back up to Norfolk on the night Hengist was killed without his workmates knowing about it. Though Janette had said she'd left immediately the rehearsal finished, perhaps she'd stayed behind for a while. And perhaps Jem had seen them together, and had killed Hengist after Janette left.

I shook my head.

That still didn't explain Zillah's presence in the churchyard.

No sooner had I said goodbye to Toots than my phone rang again.

'Hello.'

A long silence followed.

'Hello,' I said, more loudly.

'Oh, Rags. Is that you? Bert here, from Peasmarsh.'

'Hello, Bert,' I said, raising my voice. 'What can I do for you?'

'I just thought you'd like to know, the reverend is back. I saw him going into the church just now.'

I thanked him and grabbed my car keys. I had a chance to talk to the Reverend Hugh Blackthorn for the first time.

26

In which Rags meets the Reverend Hugh Blackthorn

I went first to the church, but found it locked up. Then I made my way to the vicarage a stone's throw away. The door was opened by an elderly man with spectacularly white false teeth and a head bald as an egg. When I asked if the Reverend Blackthorn was at home, he gave me a blinding smile and explained that he and his wife had bought the vicarage ten years before, 'and the reverend lives over there,' pointing at a boxy semi at the end of a row of new-build houses.

I trekked over the road. The front garden was crammed with September colour – dahlias and chrysanthemums displaying neon pink, acid-yellow and burgundy blossoms. The flower beds were a tad regimented, but the flowers felt in keeping with the man I'd seen in the photographs in the church: warm, generous, colourful.

But the Hugh who opened the door was haggard and unkempt. His thick, shoulder-length hair was unbrushed and his jeans and shirt crumpled. Granted, he still had a smudgy black eye and the remnants of a scab on one side of his forehead, but it wasn't just that. He reeked of sorrow, of regret.

I'd decided it was best to be straight with him, so I told him that I'd been commissioned to write a feature on Hengist but was also looking for Zillah, at her mother's request. He leant forward, fiddling with the hearing aid in one of his ears. I repeated what I'd said.

His eyes filled with tears. 'You'd better come in then.'

The house was clean and tidy, but a sour smell of bleach made me think that Evangeline had probably been hard at work getting the house ready for Hugh's return from hospital. Photographs of the project that I'd seen in the church also hung in the hall. In them Hugh looked radiant, relaxed, surrounded by children, his greying hair held back in a ponytail.

He led me into the lounge and offered me tea. Hovering at the kitchen door I made small talk, asking him how long he'd been in the parish (six years), and how he'd come to be involved in the African project. His doleful face lightened up a fraction as he told me that he'd recently travelled to Uganda to work on an aid project, adding, 'I was lucky that my parishioners and the diocese were happy for me to go. The three months I spent there were the most rewarding of my life.'

'Will you go back?'

His shoulders slumped. 'I doubt it. There are things that require my attention here.'

'I was so sorry to hear about your accident.'

He looked at me with dull, blue-grey eyes. Though he had strong, regular features, his face was puffy, saggy. 'Thank you. I still can't remember what happened – not unusual after a head injury.'

'And I gather you've been in hospital.'

'That's right. They kept me in for a week after my accident. Evangeline and Terry were kind enough to collect me and insisted that I stay with them overnight before I came back here.'

'She must be a great asset to the parish.'

'Indeed she is.' He carried the mugs of tea through to the lounge and said, as soon as we were seated, 'So you're looking for Zillah?'

'Yes. Her mother is very concerned about her.'

'And have you any idea where she might be? I gather from Evangeline that she left the church at short notice. I knew nothing about that until I left hospital.'

'No, but I've been in contact with all the letting agents, and made appeals on social media. I'm sure it's only a matter of time,' I replied, wondering just how much Evangeline had told him about the circumstances of Zillah's hasty departure. 'But I'm sure you'll have heard that she was seen here two nights ago, so at least we know she's alive and well.'

'Yes,' he said, his voice breathy with emotion. 'I suppose that's something.'

'I gather the two of you were close.'

His eyes burned into mine. 'She was the light of my life.' He tugged a handkerchief out of his fleece pocket and blew his nose loudly, muttering, 'I'm sorry. I'm all over the place since this head injury.'

'She can't be far away,' I said, as gently as I could. 'I promise I'll let you know as soon as I get any news.'

I sipped my tea until he'd wiped his nose and given me a watery smile. I hadn't believed Evangeline when she said that Hugh was entangled with Zillah. He was about twenty-five years older than her, for a start. But perhaps Evangeline was right. Perhaps he was in love with her.

'How long had you known her?'

'Only a few weeks. I first met her when she turned up at the church. She rang me when she was desperate to leave The Sistren, and I offered her sanctuary.'

'But I gather you knew her mother?'

He pulled a face as if I'd wafted rotten meat under his nose. 'I knew her when we both lived in Fakenham. I was a few years older than her, but we were in the same congregation and went to the same pubs.' He pulled a face. '*Julie*, she was called back then, before she decided to change her name to Julian, in honour of St Julian of Norwich. We were in the same Christian youth group, but I found her ... difficult.'

'Then why did she have your phone number?'

Hugh looked down at his hands. 'She came to me for help when she found she was pregnant. The father of her baby had disappeared, and she didn't have any close friends. She knew her parents would disown her when they found out. I'm afraid I wasn't kind. I virtually told her that she'd made her bed and would have to lie on it, and then ...' His words petered out.

'And then what?'

'I left North Norfolk, and by the time I returned she'd gone to live in Norwich.'

'But you wrote to her.'

He gave a shambolic shrug. 'Once I started studying for the priesthood I had to reflect a great deal on my earlier life, and I believed I should have done more to help her. We were both Christians, and I'd turned her away in her hour of need.'

'Julian told Zillah that she'd married the father of her child, and that he'd died in a car accident when they were living in London.'

He studied his hands again – hands that were trembling slightly. 'I know, but that's not true. That was a story she invented so her parents wouldn't disown her. As far as I know he's still alive. Julie told me Zillah's father was working on a fairground that was passing through Norfolk, and that she'd slept with him in a moment of madness.'

'Have you told Zillah?'

He said nothing.

'Doesn't she deserve to know the truth?'

'Yes, but it should come from her mother and not from me. I promised her that.'

'So you spoke to Julian?'

'Briefly. After I wrote to her, she wrote back, giving her phone number, and I rang her as part of my desire to make amends. It's always better to speak to someone than to hold them at arm's length with a letter or an email.'

'But you didn't meet her in person?'

He shook his head, looking as if he might say more, then thinking better of it. I suspected Julian had given him a piece of her mind when he telephoned, and he'd decided he'd done enough making amends.

'And did you meet Laurie, the young man who came to visit Zillah while she was at St Botolph's?'

A flame of anger lit up his face. 'No. I was away at a diocesan retreat when he turned up.'

'But Evangeline told you about him.'

He struggled to contain his feelings. 'Yes she did, and I wasn't happy about it. Evangeline said she thought he was a bad influence. In fact I tried to talk to Zillah about it, but she told me it was none of my business.'

Interesting. Perhaps their discussion was one of the times Zillah had referred to when she said that she and Hugh had argued.

'Can we talk about Hengist?' I said, deciding I'd get no more out of him about Zillah.

He jerked as if stung, then looked up with tears bright in his eyes. 'What about him?'

'Had you known him long?'

'You could say that.'

'So you were close?'

The tears that had gathered in Hugh's eyes spilled over. He pulled out a handkerchief, mopped them up and blew his nose loudly. I waited. Eventually he gave another of those shrugs. 'He asked if he could rehearse in the church hall. I wish I'd never agreed.' His face darkened. 'None of this would have happened if he hadn't used the hall for his bloody rehearsals.'

I scribbled in my notebook, puzzled by the intensity of the Reverend Hugh Blackthorn's anger.

'And can you think of anyone who might have wished to harm him? Anyone who bore him a grudge?'

'I'm afraid not. And I really don't think I can help you any more.' With a wince of pain, he got up from the sofa. 'I need to go and lie down. Sorry I'm not better company. I was told this could be one of the after-effects of the head injury.'

His face was full of sorrow. Clearly he was on some kind of emotional roller-coaster.

Poor man.

27

In which Evangeline is miffed and Betzy gloats

Evangeline Nielsen

As Evangeline pulled up outside the parish office she saw the scruffy car belonging to that woman with the daft name parked outside the church. I mean, who calls themselves Rags? The silly mare just wanted attention.

Evangeline got out of her car – a red Ford Fiesta polished to within an inch of its life – and took a hurried squizz around the churchyard.

It was empty. Just as she'd thought: Rags was probably pestering Hugh when all he needed was some peace and quiet. With storm clouds brewing in her head she marched over the road towards the front garden she'd planted to cheer him up when he went into one of his gloomy moods. But before she reached the gate the front door opened and she saw the cheeky cow squeezing Hugh's hand as if they were best friends.

Her throat filled with rage, but she swallowed it down. No way was she going to make an exhibition of herself.

Seeing her, Rags called, 'Oh I'm glad I've run into you. I wanted to ask you a few questions about the night of the rehearsal.'

'There's no point in asking me anything,' she said, marching up the path. 'I left the hall unlocked, and Hengist dropped the key back into the office. I was at home all evening. Ask Terry, my husband, if you don't believe me.'

'I just wondered if anyone had talked to you – mentioned seeing anything unusual that evening.'

'No one has, but if they did I'd go to the police. You shouldn't be meddling in things that don't concern you.'

That wiped the smile from her face, thought Evangeline as Rags came down the path with her nose in the air – stuck-up bitch – and had the cheek to say, 'thank you,' before heading back to her car.

Evangeline found Hugh flopped down on the sofa. She started tidying cushions and clearing away the empty mugs. 'I hope she didn't upset you. She shouldn't have come here worrying you like that.'

'She still doesn't know where Zillah is.'

Evangeline pressed her lips together. Here he was, going on about Zillah again! That stupid girl had turned his head. He'd been fine until she turned up, all pathetic, wanting to stay in the flat.

'You don't need to worry about her. She'll have gone off with that boyfriend of hers.'

Hugh shook his head. 'He wasn't her boyfriend.'

'I saw them together. They were on the bed.'

'I know what you saw, but he wasn't her boyfriend,' said Hugh, his voice getting louder. 'And I'll thank you to stop saying that.'

So that's how it was. He was in one of his moods.

'I've brought you a casserole,' she said, lifting up her

cloth bag with one hand. 'So you don't have to worry about cooking tonight.'

The anger drained from his face. 'That's so kind of you, Evangeline. I'm not up to much at the moment.'

'Why don't you go and have a lie down for a while?'

Meekly, he got to his feet and shuffled upstairs. She watched him go with hands on her hips. Once she heard his bedroom door close she took the casserole and some prepared vegetables through to the kitchen and put them in the fridge. Then she started her search.

It didn't take long. Within five minutes she'd found what she was looking for.

* *

Betzy Stretch

Betzy Stretch was taking a strong interest in events at St Botolph's. Stationed with her top-notch binoculars behind a tree on the other side of the village green, she watched the comings and goings from Hugh's house with amusement. She'd met Bert in the street when she was walking Monty, her Lakeland Terrier, and he'd told her that Rags was looking into Hengist's death. Ha! Betzy wouldn't meet her until she was good and ready. And when she did, she'd tell her some home truths. She wouldn't just mouth platitudes about how much Hengist had been loved and how much he'd be missed.

Because that was rubbish. The man had been pure poison. He'd had everyone running round like headless chickens, trying to gain his favour.

Everyone except her.

She was one of the few people who knew what he was really like – the damage he could do to a person. A long, long time ago he'd seduced a young, naive woman and taken everything from her: not just her self-confidence and respect. No, he'd also emptied her bank account and made her get rid of the child he'd fathered. That had sent the young woman into a dark, dark place. A decade passed before she emerged, stronger than before. He'd called her ugly, so she had work done on her face. He'd called her stupid so she studied and came out of college with a first class degree in classics. He'd called her fat, so she had an operation to shrink her stomach.

It's amazing how much a person can change if they put their mind to it. When she turned up in Peasmarsh it had been priceless to see his face when he eventually recognised her.

She was delighted he was dead.

She could have talked to that uptight police woman who went on the TV, or to Rags – and told them something which would blow all their theories apart.

But she wasn't going to do that. Not yet.

28

In which Rags seriously enjoys herself

Dave was leafing through a copy of *Mojo* when I went into The Fleece. He jumped up and offered me a drink.

'I'll have a glass of Sauvignon. Thank you.'

'Small, medium or large?'

I thought for a millisecond. 'Large.'

When he returned with the drinks – he had a pint of local bitter – I pointed at his copy of *Mojo*. 'I used to get that every month. Loved it.'

'Why did you stop?'

'Ran out of time to read it.' And funds to pay for it.

He smiled at me – that lovely, open smile. The rest of his face was nothing to write home about, but his mouth was delicious.

'Anyway,' I said. 'Tell me why you're reading *Mojo*. Are you a massive Bruce Springsteen fan? He seems to feature in every other issue.'

'Of course.'

'And Led Zep?'

'Guilty as charged. I'm a drummer, you see. And if you're a drummer you have to love the late lamented John Bonham.'

'Where's your kit?'

'In my parents' garage.' He laughed. 'When things get on top of me I go out there and thrash the drums. Very therapeutic.'

'I like a bit of Zep, but I'm a soul music fan at heart.'

'Me too.'

'I mean, listen to that drum intro on *Ain't too Proud to Beg*.'

He banged his pint on the table. 'I love that! Tried for years to get it right.'

I felt myself relax, unwind. We raved about our favourite tracks. He bought me another glass of wine and another pint for himself, insisting that he had more money than me and adding, 'I'm on my bike tonight.'

Before I got too merry, I remembered to ask him about Iain giving him a lift home from the rehearsal. He confirmed that they'd left just after 10, and added that they'd gone for a drink at The Fleece, at Iain's suggestion. 'He said he needed to unwind, and so we had a pint before he ran me home.'

'How long were you in the pub?'

'About half an hour.'

'And how well do you know him?'

'I've only met him a couple of times; he's ten years younger than me, and I was working full-time in London until my mother got ill. But I saw him act in *The Importance of Being Earnest* when I was visiting my parents once.'

'And what was he like?'

'Brilliant. Properly talented, though he was only a teenager. After that he went off the scene for a few years. I heard he was busy with A-levels and university.'

'And did he ever talk to you about his father?'

Dave thought for a moment. 'When we were in The Fleece he mumbled something about how his father was a total arsehole. I was a bit taken aback, to be honest, because I can't imagine saying anything like that about my parents.'

I sipped my drink in silence for a few seconds. 'What about Cedric?' I asked. 'Do you know when he left the church hall?'

'Same time as us. He followed us down the road to Wells.'

Ah. So I could probably count him out, too.

'Let's talk about *you*,' said Dave, leaning closer, his breath warm on my neck. 'How come you're a fan of the Tamla Motown back catalogue?'

I told him that I'd discovered a love for Tamla Motown at retro discos while I was at university. 'I collected vinyl – old singles and LPs. I wish I still had them.'

'And were you into Northern Soul?'

'To a degree. But I loved Tamla the best. Marvin Gaye and Stevie Wonder were my absolute favourites.'

As I took a few sips of Sauvignon I thought back to the night I met Matt, my long-term partner, at York University. We danced to *Let's Get it On*, went home together and spent the next decade as a couple – a gilded decade in many ways, as we both progressed in our respective careers (journalism for me and film editing and production for him). I thought we were in it for the long term.

I sighed.

'What's up?'

Strangely enough, Dave looked a bit like Matt. He had the same freckled, good-natured face, the same sandy hair that wouldn't lie flat, the same physique that would never be willowy.

I gave my head a little shake. 'Nothing, really. Tell me what you do in London a couple of days a week.'

He gave me another of those enticing smiles. 'I work on *Drums Monthly* – one of those mags for total nerds. I do everything from subbing to selling advertising. They can't afford to employ me full-time, but that's OK because I need to be around for my dad.' He paused. 'My mum's not very well.'

'I'm sorry to hear that.'

He pulled a rueful face. 'She's got early onset dementia. My dad's older than her and finding it hard to cope.'

'Oh, crap.'

'Yeah. That's about it.'

'Siblings?'

'Nope.'

He took a long swallow of beer. Outside the window a couple of gulls were squabbling over a dropped chip against the backdrop of a cloudy sky.

'But it's not so bad,' he said, his voice determined to be cheerful. 'I get to spend lots of time with them.'

We both drank in silence for a while – an easy silence, that didn't need to be rushed.

'So how come you ended up here?' he asked.

'I grew up just outside King's Lynn and moved back to Norfolk in the summer,' I said, leaving out a couple of decades, and the sad tale of how I was driven out of London by a combination of my own hubris and the vicious London culture of rising rents.

'And do you like it?'

'Love it. My dad lives in Fakenham. He came to the auditions: grey hair, neat beard, sitting with his partner Susie.'

'So he's your dad? Nice bloke.'

I paused, taking a sip of wine before asking, 'What did you think of Hengist? How did you get on with him?'

Dave thought for a moment. 'Well, it was obvious that he was a control freak, but I let that go over my head. He knew what he was doing. I was in his production of *All My Sons* – just a small role, but I enjoyed it. Much as I love my parents, it's good to get out of the house.'

'Amen to that.'

'In fact I'm putting a band together. I just need a rhythm guitarist and we can start gigging.'

'You do realise you'll have to play the Status Quo canon,' I said, only half joking. 'They're demi-gods out here.'

'I don't mind a bit of Quo.'

I leaned towards him. 'Believe it or not, I play guitar.'

'Then we should have a jam session.'

I laughed. 'I'm crap!'

'I'm sure you're not that bad.'

'Yes, I am. I love it but I'm crap.'

'Then why don't you get some lessons? My friend's a great teacher. I'll give you his number.'

Warm from the wine, I watched him slip his phone from his back pocket and scroll through his contacts. Here was a genuinely nice, positive guy, who didn't appear to have huge hang-ups. Astonishing. Yes, he was younger than me, but what was wrong with that?

A moment later, the phone number pinged into my messages. 'Thanks. Having a few lessons might motivate me to practise.'

At about eleven he said he should get going. 'But thank you for this evening.'

Wheeling his bike, he walked me up Staithe Street under a huge, luminous moon. Outside my front door he bent down and kissed me on the mouth – not a hard, intrusive kiss but a gentle, exploratory one.

I went upstairs with a smile on my face.

29

In which Rags' sweet dreams
are rudely disturbed

Yes, I had sweet dreams, but was rudely awakened by the ringing of my phone at seven. My heart did a huge thump when I saw it was Gwendolyn.

'Mum? What is it?'

No words – not even a rebuke and instruction to call her Gwendolyn.

'Are you OK?'

Just the sound of sobbing.

'Please, just tell me where you are. Do you want me to come and collect you?'

She hung up. I rang back. No joy. Rang back again. No joy: she didn't pick up. Cursing, I went up to the bathroom for a sort-of shower, using the rubber hose and kneeling in the bath. While it wasn't satisfactory, it did make me feel more refreshed.

Bloody Gwendolyn. Bloody, bloody Gwendolyn.

I dried myself off, pulled on some old jeans and a favourite purple sweatshirt and stomped downstairs to make myself some coffee. I thought of ringing Dad but decided against it. It would only upset him, and he wouldn't be able to help.

Instead I rang Toots, who'd told me she was always up with the lark. She picked up sounding cheerful as ever.

'Hello, gorgeous? What's up?'

'It's my bloody mother! She's ...' I began.

Then burst into tears.

Ten minutes later I was sitting at Toots' kitchen table, with a strong black coffee and a slice of soda bread toast in front of me.

'She announced that she was on a diet of air and water, and when I tried to tell her that was crazy, things escalated.'

Toots' hand closed over mine.

'And then I told her to bugger off and not come back.'

'Oh dear.'

I took a huge bite of buttered toast. 'She's my mother,' I continued, feeling the tears well up again, 'and I shouldn't have said that to her.'

'Don't blame yourself, sweetheart. I'm sure you've tried your best. Plus, she's an adult who should be able to look after herself.'

I spluttered. 'You must be joking. She's always had some man to look after her. First it was my dad, then Nigel, my stepfather. She's never had to lift a finger for herself.'

'She's not ...' Toots hesitated, searching for the right words. ' ... not losing her mental faculties, is she?'

'Don't think so. She's the same as she's always been – a self-centred drama queen.' I released a soggy sigh. 'And now she could be in serious trouble, and I haven't got a clue where she is. She refused to tell me.'

Toots gave my hand a pat then got up to collect some

kitchen roll so I could blow my nose.

We sat quietly for a few minutes, crunching toast and finishing our coffees.

'I've had a thought,' said Toots. 'There's a new spiritual centre opened up near Cley. Apparently it's a bit hush-hush because they haven't got proper planning permission, but they're renting an old barn. My neighbour was talking about it a few days ago.'

'Can you stay there?'

'I think she said they were putting up some yurts.'

'I can't see Gwendolyn bedding down in a yurt.'

'And a couple of luxury caravans.'

'That sounds more like her.'

Toots gave me one of her grins. 'What are we waiting for? Let's check it out.'

Five minutes later we were bowling along the coast road in Toots' vintage Triumph Herald. We wove our way through the village of Stiffkey, where Toots pointed out The Red Lion pub, saying she'd take me there for lunch one day soon. The whisper of the reed beds drifted in the open window as we sailed past the Cley Marshes Wildlife Reserve, reminding me of the times that Dad and I had walked Napoleon here. That gave me a pang: I missed them both now that Dad was involved with Susie and less often in Fakenham.

At Cley we turned off the coast road and made our way inland for a couple of miles. 'I'm sure it's somewhere round here,' said Toots, peering out of the car window after we'd gone down two narrow lanes that led nowhere in particular.

'Let's head towards Langham,' she said. 'I know there are several old barns in that area which might be what we're looking for.'

After another twenty minutes of bobbing around lanes, she gave a sigh and said that perhaps we'd better leave it for now, adding, 'I'll drop in on my neighbour later for clearer instructions. I don't have her phone number.'

I agreed that was best. Truth was, after a couple of hours with Toots, I felt much calmer. Surely my mother would have called again if she was in immediate danger.

It could all just be a huge wind-up. She'd done this sort of thing occasionally when I was a kid – disappearing and practically giving Dad a heart attack, then reappearing two days later and asking what all the fuss was about.

I was back home, preparing a report for Julian and thinking I should go along to the police incident room to report what I'd learned about Jem, when my phone rang.

It was Betzy, suggesting we meet in the Deli at eleven.

30

In which Rags is wound up by Betzy

Betzy was sitting bolt upright on a hard chair sipping a black coffee when I arrived at The Deli. As I entered, she pointedly looked at her watch. I was two minutes late because Dad had rung shortly before I left the flat, and I'd had a brief catch-up with him, omitting any mention of the latest Gwendolyn drama.

I gave her my sweetest smile. 'Sorry I'm late. Can I get you anything?'

'I haven't got long,' she replied, which I took as a coded command to sit down straightaway, without ordering.

Stuff her. I had a feeling she wanted to meet me, wanted to talk. And she could wait.

I bought an Earl Grey tea and returned to her table. 'Thank you for agreeing to meet me.'

She inclined her head as if she were some kind of duchess and I was a serving wench. What a strange fish she was: tall, big-boned, with streaked grey and blonde hair pulled back into a bun. Angular features and thin lips coloured vermillion. She was clothed entirely in black: a tailored shirt, buttoned to the neck, trousers and brogues. At the audition she'd been wearing a thirties-style dress – an Aunt Agatha sort of costume – and seeing her now in a different get-up suggested to me that her whole life was some sort of an act or pretence.

'I believe you wanted to talk to me about Hengist.'

'Yes. I'd love to get your impressions of him as a director. I'm writing a piece for the local press.'

She thought for a moment, looking at me with a smug, superior expression on her face. 'He wasn't bad, but he wasn't half as good as he thought he was. He would have been nowhere without that wife of his. She ran the company – sorted out all the finances and administration – while he took the credit.'

'So you weren't friends.'

'I didn't say that. Sometimes your best friends are those that tell you the truth.'

'So you were his friend.'

'I didn't say that either.'

What a tiresome woman. 'Can you tell me when you left the hall after the rehearsal?'

'Certainly. I left at 10 o'clock. I live in the village, so was home by five past ten.'

'Can anyone confirm that?'

A sour smile played around her lips. 'Now you're starting to sound like a police officer, which you're not, are you?'

That was a no, then.

Betzy leant forward, resting her hands on the table so she could poke her nose close to mine. 'Can we stop beating round the bush? You want to know about Hengist and I have certain information I can pass on to you.'

I pulled away from her musty breath. 'Fire away, then. I'd love to hear what you have to say'

'At a price.'

What was she up to? Her clothes were new and of good quality. She didn't look as if she needed money.

'Well?'

'I might be able to offer you something, to cover your expenses.'

'How much?'

'Fifty pounds.'

Her red lips split open into a grisly grin. 'I was thinking of five thousand.'

I blinked, wondering if I'd heard right.

'Believe me, it would be worth every penny. You see, I'm privy to information about Hengist Bright that no one else knows. What I have to say is dynamite.'

'Then why don't you go to a national newspaper?'

'That would be no fun. They wouldn't appreciate the irony of it all.'

'Or go to the police. It's against the law to withhold information that could lead to a conviction.'

'Ah, but I didn't say the information would lead to a conviction.'

She withdrew her face, and resumed her bolt-upright position. I sipped my tea. After draining my cup I said, 'I'm afraid I don't have access to five thousand pounds, and even if I did, I'd need more information before I'd consider handing over anything like that amount of money.'

'Let's just say I know something about the vicar that might help you see the case in a very different light.'

I frowned. Hugh had certainly been angry with Hengist. Perhaps their relationship was more complex than I'd assumed.

Betzy stood up, picking up a Gucci bag hanging from the back of her chair as she did so. 'And now, since you're clearly not interested, I'll bid you good day.'

And with that, she made her exit.

I decided I needed to discuss this with Toots and was scrolling through my contacts when I became aware of a man sitting on a nearby sofa watching me. When I caught his eye, he dropped his gaze. Middle-aged, he had a lined, smoker's face and a head of greying curls. His clothes were clean and ironed, but well worn – jeans going into holes at the knees, and a tweed jacket patched up at the elbows. Not unattractive, he looked rather worn down by life.

And he was paying close attention to me.

31

In which Betzy gloats again

Betzy Stretch

Betzy strolled towards her car with a smile playing round her lips. That had given the jumped-up journalist something to think about!

She'd never expected to get five grand out of her, but oh it had been fun seeing her face when she demanded it.

Because that's what this was all about: fun. Amusing herself.

Sooner or later Rags would discover the truth about what had gone on at St Botolph's church. That would be pay-off time. Of course, she, Betzy, had a pretty good idea, as she'd been watching through a pair of powerful binoculars. She hadn't been able to see everything – from her house she only had a view of the back of the churchyard – but she'd seen enough.

Oh how delicious it was when someone who was guilty got their comeuppance.

She decided to pick up some shopping while she was in Wells. The greengrocers first: plump strawberries, figs, Jersey royal potatoes, asparagus. Then the butcher's for the best cut of steak: she liked a good slice of red meat once a week.

After she'd picked up her shopping, she made her way to the royal blue Audi convertible parked on the quay. It was one of her little vanities to park where people could gawp at her, wondering how a woman like her came to drive a car like that. They probably thought her husband had bought it for her.

Ha! That was a joke. She'd never found a man who was her equal. Most of them were self-centred popinjays who thought they were the centre of the universe.

The first had been the worst.

* *

Mindy Bright

Mindy stretched her arms above her head, untying the knots in her shoulders. She'd been hard at work for four hours on a report needed by an Italian company who were starting up a pre-loved designer clothing business.

Work was good. Work distracted her from dwelling on the evening Hengist had died. If only the flight hadn't been cancelled. Everything would have been different if she'd been on that bloody plane to Budapest.

A spurt of guilt ran through her, making her feel physically sick.

A knock on her office door quelled the nausea.

'Mum? I need to talk to you.'

Mindy gave her head a little shake. Time to stop being self-indulgent: her son needed her.

'Can I come in?'

'Of course.'

The door opened slowly. Iain had always been like that – cautious, watchful, fearful of danger. She suppressed a spark of irritation. Though she loved her son, she wished he wasn't such a flake.

'What is it, darling?'

'I need you to honour the agreement I had with Dad.'

Noticing his greasy hair, the smell of unwashed clothes and stale cigarettes, she told herself to be patient with him.

'The production isn't going ahead, so the agreement is no longer binding,' she said, as gently as she could.

'But he *promised*,' said Iain, on the verge of tears.

'I know, but ...'

'And I need money. I need it now.'

Something snapped in Mindy. 'Just stop it, will you? Your father's died, and all you can whine about is money! You get a generous allowance – far more than most boys of your age. Why can't you grow up and take responsibility for yourself?'

A horrible silence filled the space between them before Iain turned and thundered down the stairs. In a flash Mindy was on her feet and running after him.

'I'm sorry, darling. I didn't mean to ...'

But before she could catch up with him he'd run out of the front door, got into his car and roared away up the drive.

Mindy closed her eyes for a moment, forcing back the tears. She'd been too harsh with him: he was grieving, too. He and Hengist had been fighting for years, but she knew that he loved his father underneath all that. When he was a kid and Hengist had smaller ambitions, they'd spent dreamy holidays in a static caravan on the Pinewoods Holiday Park. She often wished those days back, when she had a part-time job in a friendly IT company, and Hengist had no idea how rich her father was.

She pulled out her phone and sent Iain a text: *I'm sorry I flew off the handle. I'm always here for you. Let's talk when you get back. Love you. Mum X*

Finding refuge in work, as she always did, she returned to her desk and read through the report on the Italian start-up company, checking the figures, making sure there were no typos.

And then an idea came into her head. Perhaps this tragic situation gave her the opportunity to do something she'd wanted to do for a long, long time.

32

In which Rags visits the grieving widow

I was sitting at the table, typing up another report for Julian when my phone rang.

'This is Mindy. I gather you're writing a tribute to my dead husband.'

'Yes, I ...'

'I'd like to talk to you. Come over as soon as you're free.'

I agreed to drive over there right away.

Mindy was waiting for me at the front door, and led me through to the lounge with the unappealing but expensive black and white prints. After I'd offered my condolences, she thanked me, and held out some stapled sheets of paper.

'Here. This is a list of the productions Hengist has directed for The Peasmarsh Players, along with the excellent reviews they received. His CV is at the back. You'll see that he taught at a local college for some years: he's always had a huge interest in supporting his local community.'

'And what sort of man was he? What were his special qualities?' I asked, pulling out my notebook.

'He was a man of unique vision and rare talent. A man of intelligence and charm.'

Well, that's one way of putting it, I thought, scribbling shorthand notes.

'And he contributed immeasurably to the success of The Peasmarsh Players. Ask anyone: they'll say the same.'

I looked up. Her face was pale, her eyes bloodshot despite the disguise of eye-liner and mascara, but she was composed. 'I came along to the first rehearsal and could see how important he was to the company.' I paused. 'You, too.'

She shrugged. 'I helped with the admin, but he was the driving force. We'll miss him terribly.'

'How long had you been married?'

'Twenty-five years. We met in London. He was a lecturer at the college where I was doing business studies. We hit it off immediately.'

I kept my head bowed: so here was another example of Hengist moving in on a younger woman. But, in Mindy's case, he'd met his match. She'd obviously refused to be consigned to the list of love-em-and-leave-em conquests.

She cleared her throat. 'Anyway: there's something else I want to raise with you. I gather from my son that you were asking about the night when Hengist died.'

'Yes.'

'And I've discovered that you're a private investigator as well as a journalist.'

'Yes. I've been looking into the disappearance of Zillah, the young woman who was staying at St Botolph's church.'

'May I ask why you don't just leave these matters to the police?'

I thought for a moment then decided to be straight with her. 'Zillah's mother is concerned that the police suspect her daughter of killing Hengist. She wants me to find evidence to prove otherwise. If I discover anything material to the investigation, I'll take it to the police.'

She let a pause hang in the air for a moment. 'I might be able to help you there.'

I held my pencil above the paper. Interesting.

'You've probably found out that my plane to Budapest that night was cancelled, so I came back to Norfolk and decided to surprise Hengist by taking him for a drink after the rehearsal. By the time I arrived – about twenty-five past ten – the rehearsal was over and the hall locked up, but his car was still there, so I went into the churchyard. He often took a stroll there to clear his head after rehearsals.'

She came to a halt. 'Yes?' I asked, not entirely convinced that Hengist mooched around the churchyard to unwind.

'What I'm about to tell you now is confidential, and is not to go into any feature you write. Do you agree?'

'Of course.'

'I heard raised voices – Hengist and a woman – coming from the church porch and hurried round there. At first I couldn't see who the woman was, but she was shouting at him, telling him he was the scum of the earth.' She took a breath for dramatic effect. 'And it looked like she had something like a stone in one hand.'

'So did you go and break up the quarrel?'

'No. When she saw me she ran away. I went up to him and asked what on earth was happening. He said it was nothing – a storm in a teacup, arising from the rehearsal. He said something like, 'I've put somebody's nose out of joint.' He said he'd sort it out and suggested I head home, as I had an early start. But I knew it was something more serious. You see, I recognised the woman, and I knew he had unfinished business with her – something from way, way back, before we met.'

She paused. I looked at her.

'It was Betzy. Betzy was the woman he was arguing with.'

I didn't get much more out of her. She wouldn't divulge the 'unfinished business', saying that it was confidential, and insisted that she'd slept in the spare room that night as she had to be up at 3 am, and so wasn't aware that Hengist hadn't come in the night before. 'And we park our cars in separate garages, so I didn't realise his car was missing when I left early the next morning.' I told her she should pass on the information about Betzy to the police. She said she intended to do so as soon as I'd left, adding, 'but I thought it was only fair to let you know, too.'

I felt I needed to chew things over with someone else, so rang Toots, inviting her for brunch. I filled her in on my recent meetings, and we concluded that I needed to report what I knew about Jem's van being seen in Peasmarsh to the police. We both agreed that Mindy's story about Betzy threatening Hengist sounded unlikely, to say the least.

'But Betzy's weird. She's up to something,' I said.

'And for all we know Mindy could have been the one who attacked Hengist, in a jealous rage.'

I shook my head. 'Having met her today, I can't believe that. But I do think there are things she's not telling us.'

After coffee, toast and scrambled eggs we got out pens and paper and updated the list of suspects I'd drawn up a couple of days before.

1. **Alfie Adams** – *He was furious with Hengist for not giving him the part of Bertie Wooster. he left the Eddie around 10 pm, but no one has yet come forward who saw him at St Botolph's. His remark that he wanted to kill Hengist was probably just hot air.*

2. **Jem Townley** – *jealous of Hengist, and probably suspected him of demanding sexual favours from Janette. Did he drive*

back from his carpentry job in Sussex and find Hengist and Janette kissing and kill Hengist in a fit of uncontrolled rage and jealousy? Andrea thinks she saw his van there around 10.00 pm, but this has not been confirmed.

3. **Mindy Bright** – *Did she find out about Hengist's latest infidelity and snap? She admits she was at St Botolph's at 10.25 pm.*

4. **Janette Tinker** – *Says she walked home, leaving at 10 pm, but only her mother can back up her story, and her mother would probably be happy to lie for her. Did she attack him because he kept demanding sexual favours?*

5. **Zillah Lloyd** – *Zillah was at the church at 10.15 – seen and heard by Bert. There's no doubt that she had an argument with Hengist. Had Hengist made sexual advances to her? Was she angry with him because of that? Her whereabouts are still unknown, but her appearance at the church suggests she's probably still in the local area. A history of rages when younger.*

6. **Betzy Stretch** – *She hated Hengist and was not sorry that he died. Did he seduce her and/or let her down in the past? Though Mindy has said she saw Betzy arguing with Hengist, no one has corroborated this.*

We left Iain and Dave off the list for now, as they'd left together at just after 10, and provided each other with an alibi for the next forty minutes, though it was possible that one or both of them returned to the church at a later point. Cedric had left the rehearsal at 10, and so was probably out of the picture, too. Though he clearly hadn't wanted to play the role of Jeeves, I couldn't believe that was a strong enough motive to kill Hengist.

Looking at our notes, I sighed. I felt like I was wading through porridge. And I still hadn't found Zillah.

'Come on,' I said to Toots. 'Let's head off to the incident room. It's time we let the police loose on Jem.'

'You don't believe he did it, do you?'

'No. But we need to tell the police what we know.'

In the incident room on Polka Road I found DS Williams holding the fort. He was the officer who'd been kind to me when I was trying to unravel a mysterious death earlier in the year – much kinder than DI Chloe Cooper, who suffered from a charm deficit. He invited us into a small interview room and listened carefully when we told him Andrea had seen Jem's van – or one very like it – close to St Botolph's on the night Hengist died.

'Do you have her contact details?'

'She's the daughter of a man who lives in the sheltered housing adjoining the churchyard.' I gave him Bert's telephone number. 'She drops in to see her father most days, so he'll be able to get a message to her.'

'There'll be some CCTV we can check: I know the pub has security cameras. You say Jem Townley's van is distinctive?'

'Very. He has a hammer and saw on the side and back, and his name in large letters.'

'He's a local lad, isn't he? The name's familiar.'

'Yes,' said Toots. 'I believe he lives on the housing estate close to the East Quay. And there's something else, too. I think I saw him later that night, outside my house, in a blood-stained shirt. But I didn't get a good look at the man's face, so couldn't swear to it.'

DS Williams clicked his pen and stood up. 'Thank you for coming in, ladies. We'll certainly look into this.'

'Have you heard from Mindy, Hengist's widow? I know she also had something to report to you.'

He nodded slowly. 'Yes. She came in to make a statement this morning.'

'And is Zillah still a suspect?'

'All I can say is that we're following up several lines of investigation.'

Though his face was expressionless, something in his eyes told me that he was not convinced she was the murderer.

That gave me hope.

33

In which Dad and Napoleon offer Rags some much needed TLC

I wrote a brief report for Julian when I got home, then I sat and worried for a while.

About Gwendolyn.

Toots had told me that her neighbour was away for a couple of nights, and so she still didn't know the exact location of the barn where Gwendolyn might be getting her spiritual fix. I was tempted to head off and drive round the lanes close to Cley. The barn and yurts couldn't be *that* hard to find, could they?

On the other hand, Gwendolyn hadn't told me she was in danger. Yes, she'd been crying, but she hadn't sounded in pain, or begged for help. I was still turning all this over when the doorbell rang. My heart jolted.

But when I opened the window looking down on Staithe Street, I heard a joyful bark, and saw two familiar faces smiling up at me. Dad and Napoleon.

I ran down the stairs to open the door.

'We've come to see how you're getting on.'

I threw my arms around him. He did his thing of patting me awkwardly on the back and saying, 'There, there.'

'Thanks, Dad,' I muttered, into his shoulder.

'Napoleon and I thought you might like to go for a walk through Pinewoods. We can chat as we go.'

So I dashed upstairs to grab a cardigan, in case the sun went in, and headed round to Dad's Mini.

We parked, strolled past the pond and followed the sandy path that runs through the woods parallel to the coast. As we walked, I updated him on my search for Zillah and my attempt to find out who'd murdered Hengist.

'I feel I'm getting nowhere.'

'Come on, now. You've discovered important information about Jem, and though you haven't found Zillah, you've done everything you can. You can't perform magic, you know.'

Napoleon gave a little bark, showing that he agreed with Dad.

Dad sighed. 'And you've had the worry of having your mother staying with you.'

I walked along in silence, wondering how much to say about Gwendolyn's latest antics.

'Is there something you're not telling me?' said Dad, sounding stern.

And then it all came out: the twaddle about living off water, our row, the sobbing phone call. 'I know I should be more patient,' I concluded, 'but she drives me up the wall. One moment we're having a sensible conversation, and the next we're in the middle of an argument. And on top of it all, I'm worried about her.'

Dad's *Hmmmm* said it all.

'So, do you have any advice?' I asked, as we started to descent the steps to the beach at the end of the sandy track through the woods.

'Your mother's more resilient than she looks. Under that mystic exterior she's tough as old boots. I suggest you put your energies towards finishing the work for Julian, and trust that Gwendolyn will return when she's good and ready. She said she was going on a retreat for a few days, didn't she?'

'Yes, but ...'

'Then wait and see if she turns up at your flat. And if she doesn't, we'll put our heads together.'

At the bottom of the wooden steps, our feet sank into soft sand. Dad reached for my hand and squeezed it.

'I know you've been worried about me,' he continued, 'and I was rattled when Gwendolyn turned up. But Susie and I have been talking about the situation and I feel I can cope with it a bit better now.' He gave me one of his sweetest smiles. 'Right. Let's get down to the water and throw some sticks for Napoleon. I know he's dying to have a dip.'

As we walked towards the sea, Napoleon bounded ahead, running round the beach huts, looking for interesting smells. I'd been amazed to hear the prices these huts fetched these days: you could buy two terraced houses in Liverpool for what it cost to buy one of these bijou shacks.

We spent the next hour strolling towards Burnham Overy Staithe, throwing sticks into the waves for Napoleon, and catching up on our latest news. When I asked Dad how things were going with Susie he blushed and said they were pretty good, 'though I've been a grumpy old man for so long that I have to try to behave.'

I laughed and squeezed his arm. Yes, he'd been a grumpy old man for decades – neither of us was going to deny that. But he'd changed.

And so had I.

As we were walking back to the car through the woods, my phone rang.

'Yes?'

'It's Marianne, from A Place to Call Home. You rang about Zillah.'

'Thanks for calling me back. I was just wondering whether you'd seen anything of Zillah since we met up'

''Fraid not. But I'll ask around in case anyone else has seen her in Norwich.'

'Thanks. I've drawn a blank here.'

'No response to your social media posts?'

'No – but she was seen at the church on the night of the murder.'

Marianne gave a long whistle of surprise.

'And now the police want to talk to her.'

'They can't think she had anything to do with it.'

'She was seen arguing with Hengist Bright.'

Marianne went quiet for a minute or so, then said, 'We haven't seen Laurie for the past fortnight.'

'Do you think the two of them could be together?'

A pause, then, 'Yes. They were fond of each other and she sounds as if she needed a loyal friend.'

I thanked her and hung up. The news that Laurie had gone AWOL gave me a nasty feeling. What if Zillah was being drawn into drug use? I don't have an ethical problem with drugs – I'm fond of wine, after all – but an addiction limits a person's life – and Zillah had only just started living.

On impulse, I turned to Dad. 'Do you fancy doing a bit of detecting? I'd like to go back to the church to see if there's anything I missed.'

Dad stopped dead and looked at me. 'I thought you'd never ask. Susie's gone to her sister's in London for a few days, so I'm at your disposal.' Then, gruff and a little embarrassed, 'I'm always here for you, you know.'

As often in September, North Norfolk was at its most beautiful. Afternoon light gilded the fields, and blackberries were plumping up in the hedgerows. The trees were still clothed in dark green leaves which sighed and sang in the breeze as we bowled towards Peasmarsh in Dad's car. Napoleon was on my knee, with his paws resting on the dashboard.

This was more like it.

We went first to the church porch, opening the chicken wire gate installed to stop birds getting in there. The porch was cool, fragrant from a bunch of dried grasses someone had placed on the shelf in an earthenware jug. I remembered from the news report that Hengist had been found a few feet away from the porch, and I was glad of that. I didn't want to think of this peaceful place being sullied by such a violent act. I got down on my hands and knees and poked around under the bench that ran along one side of the porch. Napoleon dived under there and sniffed around, too. I found nothing. Dad, meanwhile, was looking through the notices pinned to the board, and investigating the shelf on which the jug was standing. He turned and shook his head.

'Nothing.'

'Let's have a look round the churchyard.'

We went outside and started a thorough search around the churchyard, though I didn't hold out much hope, since I was sure the police would have carried out a detailed search of the crime scene. Napoleon darted this way and that, getting in on the act.

Then he stuck his nose in a clump of brambles growing near the churchyard gate and started wagging his tail. He turned and barked.

'Come on! He's found something.'

Dad and I hurried over. Dad took a handkerchief from his pocket, wrapped it round his hand to protect it from thorns and gingerly manoeuvred his arm into the brambles. After a bit of twisting and turning, and much encouragement from Napoleon, his fingers closed round the object that had caused Napoleon such excitement.

It was a pregnancy test.

And it explained a hell of a lot.

34

In which Jem's afternoon off is disturbed

Jem Townley

Jem finished work a little early – he'd been doing a small job repairing a sash window – and came home to the delicious smell of his mum's baking. He found her in the kitchen tidying away the flour, butter and eggs.

'I'm making us a sponge cake. I was due some time off, and decided to come home and bake us a little treat.' Her broad face, like his but softer, creased into a smile.

'You've got flour on your chin.'

Bobbing over to the mirror, she grinned and wiped it off with a tea-towel. 'So I have.'

Watching her, he wondered, with a sickening sense of guilt, whether she'd sensed that he was planning to leave Wells. He hadn't said a word to her, but they'd always been close; she could tell when he was worried, or out of sorts.

His dad hadn't been around for years: he was living with a younger woman two streets away, and Jem hardly saw him, though they worked in the same trade. He'd moved out when Jem was ten, saying he deserved another chance in life. Complete rubbish. He just wanted to shag a younger woman and was prepared to dump his wife of twenty years to get it.

'Do you want to scrape out the bowl?'

She was holding out the mixing bowl – one of those old-fashioned ones, cream and white. All his childhood he'd rushed to scrape the cake mixture from that bowl, loving the creamy taste of butter and sugar, sometimes flavoured with a dash of coffee, vanilla or chocolate. The wooden spoon was there to be licked too.

Taking the bowl from her, he brought the spoon to his mouth. The plain, innocent taste of it made him suddenly tearful, so he had to pretend to clear his throat and bend busily over the bowl as he chased the last whirls of cake mixture.

'Is everything all right, Jem-Jem?'

He forced a smile on to his face. 'Of course. I've just had a lot on my mind – a big job I need to cost. Some pub along the coast, near Kelling. They want me to rebuild the bar.' This at least was true. He'd been looking forward to taking it on and regretted the fact that he might not be able to do it now.

'The business is doing well, then?'

'Yes,' he said, handing the bowl back to her.

'I'm proud of you – you're twice the man your father is,' she said, rinsing out the bowl and putting it into the dishwasher.

Here we go again. He wished his mum would change the record. Thirteen years after Dad left she still went on about him all the time. If she could just think about something else, she might find herself a new boyfriend.

And then he wouldn't feel so guilty about leaving.

She made them both a cup of tea while he went upstairs to shower and change. When he came down the fragrant aroma of baking sponge filled the tidy lounge where his mum was sitting doing a crossword. A selfish thought crossed his mind; he'd miss his mum's cooking when he left. Janette couldn't boil an egg. Of the two of them, he was the better cook. He'd just started on his cup of tea when the door bell rang. His mum got up to answer the door, and he almost choked when he heard the words, 'Police. We'd like a word with your son.'

With shaking fingers Jem pulled out his phone and sent Janette a hasty message. He'd just slipped the phone back in his pocket when the two police officers came through to the dining room. One of them introduced himself as DS Williams, adding, as he pointed to a tight-faced blonde woman, 'And this is DI Cooper. We'd like a word with you, please.'

'Me? I haven't been caught speeding, have I?' he said, keeping his voice light despite the thudding of his pulse.

'Your name has come up in connection with a crime.'

Jem swallowed down the lump of fear in his throat.

'We'd like you to come with us to the station,' said the blonde woman.

'Can't we talk here?' he managed.

'There's some CCTV footage we'd like you to look at.'

Suddenly Jem felt sick. Were there security cameras at the church? He hadn't seen any – in fact he was sure there were none, because Evangeline, the sour parish secretary, had been talking about having some put in when he went over to repair the damaged door of the parish office.

'We'd be grateful if you could come along with us now, Sir,' said DI Cooper, keeping her eyes fixed on Jem in a way that made his skin crawl.

'Of course.' Jem stood up. 'It's all right, Mum; I won't be long.'

35

In which Janette comes clean to Rags

Janette sounded rattled – very rattled – when she rang me.

'There's things I need to tell you. Can I come round now?'

Five minutes later she was in my sitting room, her face pale and tense.

'Jem's at the police station. They think he had something to do with the murder.'

'Wow. Sorry to hear that,' I said, trying to give no indication that I was the person who'd brought him to their attention.

'And ...' She dropped her head into her hands, starting to shake with sobs.

'And?' I said gently.

Through her cupped hands came indistinct words: 'He was in Norfolk the night of the murder,' she said, before she burst into full-blown weeping.

I got her some tissues and poured her a glass of water. After a minute or so she dabbed her eyes and blew her nose.

'And he's just sent me a text asking me to say he was with me that night. But he wasn't.'

'Do you want to tell me the whole story?'

'That's just it. I don't know the whole story. Jem's been lying to me. He swore he was in Sussex the night Hengist was killed, but now he says he drove back to Norfolk on a whim. But he never came to see me. So he must have been up to something, mustn't he?'

'Not necessarily.'

'He'd got a bee in his bonnet about Hengist, saying he was taking advantage of me.'

'And was he?'

'Not like that.' She gave a big sigh. 'Hengist wasn't looking for sex – not from me, in any case.' She fell silent.

'So what did he want?'

After pulling a face she continued, 'He wanted me to go out on dates with one of the judges of the competition, to make sure we won this time – some sleazy businessman who'd written a crap play about a hundred years ago. I had to flatter him, flirt with him – that sort of crap.'

'Was that what you'd been discussing with Hengist when I picked you up that day?'

'Yes. And he said that if I went through with it, he'd arrange for one of his agent friends from London to come and see me in the production.'

'Did you believe him?'

'Yes. He was an arrogant git, but he kept his word.' She gave another sigh. 'So I went out for lunch with this creepy old guy who spent the whole time ogling my tits and putting his hand on my leg.'

I winced. 'So do you think Jem got wind of this, and confronted Hengist?'

Janette's beautiful face crumpled into a frown. 'I don't know. I really don't know.' We sat in silence for a while then

I asked her if she thought Hengist was blackmailing anyone else involved with the production.

She was thoughtful for a moment, then replied, 'Hengist had something on Iain. You could see Iain really didn't want to be there. Same with Cedric. Hengist had somehow persuaded him to take on the part of Jeeves.'

'But you don't know how he did it?'

She shook her head. 'No. When I first joined the company Cedric got all the lead parts and loved it.'

'And then something changed?'

'Yes. But I don't know what. You could see he wasn't that keen to do *All My Sons*, but I thought maybe that was because he thought Alfie would probably make a balls-up of his part.' A faint smile crept over her face. 'You should have seen Hengist's face after Alfie forgot to make his entrance in Act Three.' Her smile vanished. 'What am I going to do about Jem?'

'I can't help you with that.'

Pulling her shoulders back, she looked me in the eye. 'Jem's really important to me, but I'm not going to jeopardise my career for him. Is that selfish?'

'No. It's called putting yourself first.'

For the first time I wondered if Jem was going to take the journey with her.

As Janette ran down the stairs I thought to myself that I had at last made a little progress. I was certain she'd told me the truth: she wasn't having an affair with Hengist and had no motive to kill him. I'd also learned that Jem was almost certainly in Norfolk on the night Hengist was killed, and that he was probably at St Botolph's at some point in the evening.

Just when, I didn't yet know.

36

In which the tension mounts

Betzy Stretch

After her little chat with the police Betzy roared along the road to Peasmarsh laughing out loud. It had been so satisfying to shoot down Mindy's ridiculous accusations. Did that stuck-up automaton in wonky clothes really think she could outwit her? In some ways it was satisfying to see that she was rattled. She must have worked out that Hengist and Betzy had a past.

Betzy had CCTV in her house – a sensible precaution for a woman living on her own in a valuable property. The CCTV footage clearly showed that she was at home, doing *The Telegraph* cryptic crossword at the time Hengist was murdered.

She hadn't had to do a thing.

* *

Mindy Bright

The phone call Mindy received from DI Cooper was chilly but nothing she couldn't deal with. Mindy politely said that she must have been mistaken, but had felt it was her citizen's duty to report what she thought she'd seen. Yes, she'd seen a figure who looked like Betzy arguing with her husband. Yes, she thought the figure had a rock in one hand. But it was dark – a cloudy night with only a sliver of moon hiding in the murk – and so she couldn't be 100 percent sure of the identity of the attacker.

'But you're sure it was a woman?'

Mindy paused, hesitating as if thinking over what she'd seen. 'Yes,' she said finally, happy to cast the blame on another female who should have known better. 'And I have another thought about who it might have been.'

* *

Janette Tinker

Janette was serving a gluey chocolate brownie in the Deli when the call came through from the police. A nasty shock ran through her bones.

As soon as it was her lunch break she headed down to the incident room, determined to get all this over with once and for all. She had a life to lead, a career to pursue, and she wasn't going to let this crap get in her way.

The police officer who interviewed her looked like he hadn't slept for a week. With him was a blonde woman who introduced herself as DI Cooper. They asked her if she could confirm that she went straight home after the rehearsal.

'Yes. And my mum can vouch for me. We watched an old episode of *Blackadder* before we went to bed.'

The two officers exchanged a glance. DS Williams made

a few notes and yawned.

'Thank you for coming in,' said the woman. 'You can go now.'

'What's this about? Did someone tell you I stayed behind?'

'I'm afraid we can't divulge that.'

Once outside, Janette swore under her breath. What the hell was going on?

She couldn't wait to get out of this one-horse town.

* *

Evangeline Nielsen

Shoving the Hoover along the hall, Evangeline tutted at the crisps and peanuts trampled into the carpet. Never the most tidy, he was turning into a complete slob. The kitchen sink was full of dirty plates and mugs. A pizza box had been thrown on the living-room floor, its lid open on smears of grease and tomato. Half a slice of garlic bread was stuck to the sofa cushion whose cover she'd washed only the week before. The house smelled of stale food and cigarette smoke.

And something else.

With a jangle in her heart she rooted around the sofa and armchair and pulled open the drawers of the little desk that sat in the corner. Nothing. On her hands and knees, she peered under the sofa. Nothing. Going through to the kitchen she had a thorough search of the kitchen cupboards. Nothing.

Then it came to her. She went out of the back door and marched down to the small garden shed.

Bingo.

The blood pounded in her head. After all she'd done for him – all he'd promised. This was a betrayal. And she didn't like a betrayal. She'd been patient with him, had shown him nothing but Christian love. She'd prayed for and with him.

They'd shared holy communion.

She'd even agreed to lie for him.

When he came back from wherever he was – he'd taken to tramping off on long walks without telling her where he was going – she'd have it out with him – get him to confess what he'd been up to.

It was for his own good.

37

In which Rags, Dad and Napoleon make a discovery

I didn't sleep well. The possible suspects for Hengist's murder were turning round in my head, and I had heard nothing more from Gwendolyn. Was she all right? Was she having some sort of mental health crisis? Was she still starving herself?

At about nine I was pottering around the flat, not quite knowing what to do with myself, when my phone rang.

It was Dad, sounding excited. 'I think I've worked out where Zillah is hiding. Meet me at the Buttlands in 20 minutes.'

And then he hung up.

Dad was in a mischievous mood when he pulled up in his Mini. Leaning over, he opened up the passenger door. 'This was Napoleon's idea, by the way. Jump in.'

As we turned into Beach Road, the penny dropped. Of course: the chalets.

But no: after we'd sailed past the entrance to Pinewoods

and parked in the car park, Napoleon scooted towards the closest flight of wooden steps leading to the beach.

'The beach huts,' I cried, wondering why it had taken me so long.

'Elementary, my dear Watson.'

At the top of the steps we stood for a few moments looking towards the distant waves and gleaming channels.

Dad turned to me, his face lit by autumn sun. 'I remembered that Napoleon was particularly interested in one of the huts the last time we were here. Let's take a look. Napoleon? Search.'

With a bark, Napoleon ran on ahead, nose down, stopping sometimes by the steps that led up to each beach hut, sniffing at the wooden supports that lifted them above the sand. Within a few minutes we'd reached the end of the row. Before us the beach and dunes stretched to Holkham and beyond. Napoleon flopped on to the soft sand, a little deflated, it seemed to me.

'Don't worry. He just needs to have another go,' said Dad, bending down and stroking Napoleon's ears. 'Good boy. Good boy. Now, I want you to find. Find Zillah.'

As he spoke, Dad looked intently into Napoleon's eyes, and I swear the little dog understood him, for he stood up and started to circle the huts once more. We walked slowly back the way we had come, going up the steps to each empty hut and trying the door.

They were either locked or padlocked.

My heart sank. I'd been sure Dad was right about Zillah hiding out here, but perhaps she'd already moved to another sanctuary.

Then I heard a sharp volley of barks from Napoleon and looked across to see him scratching at the door of a hut with peeling blue paint. Dad and I rushed over and up the steps. When I looked closely I could see that the padlock was not attached to the catch, and when I tried the door I realised it was bolted from inside. Napoleon's barks got louder. I was sure I heard quiet voices from inside.

'We know you're in there. Please open up.'

Nothing – except perhaps the sound of someone being shushed.

'If you don't open up we'll telephone the police and they'll come and arrest you.'

We waited. A short while later a bolt was pulled across and a young man with dishevelled brown hair appeared in the doorway. His face was bony, angular, with worry lines written on his forehead though he couldn't have been more than in his late twenties. His accent, when he spoke, suggested he'd been through the public school system. It certainly lacked the lazy drawl of Norfolk. 'I don't know who you are, but you're on private property. Go away.'

'Laurie?' A flicker of surprise ran across his face before he could stop it. 'I know who you are. And I know that Zillah's in there. Please let me speak to her. She needs help.'

He dithered for a moment before a voice crept out of the gloom at the back of the hut – a tired, breathy voice. 'Let her in.'

Slow, reluctant, Laurie opened the door wide enough for me to enter. Zillah was sitting on the cushioned bench that ran across the width of the hut with a blanket wrapped around her. Though fully dressed in skirt, shirt and jumper, she looked pale and shivery, her hair in straggles and her eyes dark pools.

'I've been worried about you.'

'I don't know why. You've only met me once.'

'You need to see a doctor.'

Her mouth formed itself into the stubborn line I recognised from before. 'No I don't. I'm perfectly healthy. It's just a bit cold in here.'

'You need help,' I repeated, 'for yourself and the baby.'

She flinched. 'What are you talking about?'

'I think you've been having an affair with Hengist, that you found out you were pregnant and went to the church that night to tell him.' Her head dropped forward but she said nothing. 'I'm right, aren't I?'

'What makes you think I'm pregnant?'

'The pregnancy test. You took it to show him, didn't you?'

She gave me a peculiar, shuttered look.

'And you got into an argument with him.'

'No, I didn't.'

'You were seen and heard.'

'It wasn't an argument: it was more of a discussion.'

'The police are looking for you. You know that, don't you?'

'Of course I do. I'm not stupid.'

'And when they find you, they're going to ask you some tough questions.'

Her shoulders hunched and her head sank down again.

I moved closer and sat down on the bench beside her. 'I don't believe you killed him. And if you'll help me, perhaps I can find out who did.'

'My mother put you up to this, didn't she?'

'Yes.' No point in denying it.

'And you're going to tell my mother where I am, aren't you?'

'I'm going to tell her you're safe. I think *you* should tell her where you are, when you're ready.'

Dad's voice came from the doorway. 'Can I come in?' After a moment, without waiting for an answer, he came slowly in the door. 'Hello. I'm Graham – Rags' dad.'

The smell of a match being struck and the sweet scent of roll-up tobacco smoke told me that Laurie was lighting up outside. Napoleon trotted across the floor towards me, nails clicking on the wooden boards. With a fluid leap, he jumped onto my lap and curled up there, his nose pointing towards Zillah.

'This is Napoleon. Don't worry: he doesn't bite.'

A weak smile appeared on Zillah's face. 'I always wanted a dog but Mum would never let me have one. She said they were dirty.'

Napoleon wriggled until his head found its way onto Zillah's lap. After a short hesitation she started to stroke him and I felt her body relax a little.

'I've got an idea,' said Dad. 'Why doesn't Zillah come and stay in my spare room for a few days? That way she can be safe and warm. You can tell her mother she's safe, and Zillah can decide whether she wants to see her.'

Zillah looked up, tears in her eyes. 'Would you really do that for me?'

'Of course I would. I've got a spare room sitting there doing nothing, and I don't like to see a girl in your condition living like this.'

'What about Laurie?'

Dad crossed his arms. 'I'm sorry. I'm sure he's a good lad, but he's a drug user, and I can't have that in the house.'

'He's trying to stop. I know he is.'

'Well then he might be better off where he can get some proper help.'

'There is no proper help,' came Laurie's voice from the doorway. 'All the rehab programmes have been cut. And in any case I've tried that before, and it didn't work.'

'I won't go there without you.'

'Don't be so bloody stupid. I can go back to Norwich. I'll be fine.'

'The drugs paraphernalia at St Botolph's – that was yours, wasn't it?' I asked.

He nodded, adding, 'I'd left it there the last time I visited Zillah.'

I turned to Zillah. 'Why did you leave the flat at St

Botolph's when you did? Evangeline says you had a fight with Laurie.'

She took a sharp in-breath. 'That old cow always had it in for me. I left because someone broke in at night and threatened me. A man. I don't know who it was because he was wearing a mask and had disguised his voice, but he told me that he'd do me serious harm unless I left and didn't come back.'

'Why didn't you tell me this? You could have rung me.'

'Why do you think? I was terrified.' She groaned and shifted on the bench. 'Look, I'm feeling like death warmed up. Can we go somewhere comfortable before you ask me any more questions?'

Ten minutes later we were sitting in my lounge. Zillah had her hands round a mug of camomile tea and was nibbling on a slice of toast and marmite. Already she looked warmer, brighter. She and Laurie had parted on my doorstep with a huge hug; he said he had to get back to Norwich, and there was a touch of relief on her face as he hurried up the street to the bus stop.

'Can you tell me a bit more about your relationship with Laurie?' I asked.

Her face softened. 'He's a sweetheart. He's had a huge crush on me ever since I met him. And he's totally sound: I knew he'd never tell anyone where I was, so I rang him from St Botolph's one day when I was feeling lonely, and he dropped everything to come and cheer me up.'

'This was a few weeks back?'

'Yes. He's been back a few times; we go for a walk, or meet for a coffee.'

'Evangeline thought you were an item. She says she saw you both lying on the bed.'

'We were messing around. We'd been laughing so hard we ran out of breath. He's my *friend*. We've never slept together. And after I ran away from the church I rang him and he came as soon as he could. He found us this beach hut and has been looking after me – buying food, charging our phones, getting water. I don't know what I'd have done without him.'

'And you've been giving him money?'

'I know he spends some of it on drugs, but he has to. He's an addict.' Her eyes held mine. 'But he's been cutting down since we've been in the beach hut.' Her hand closed round the crucifix hanging round her neck. 'I still have my faith, you know, and at the heart of Christianity is charity and forgiveness. I don't want him getting into trouble with the police.'

'What puzzles me,' said Dad, 'is why this man broke in and terrorised you.'

Zillah shrugged thin shoulders. 'I've been over it again and again. I just can't work it out. First I thought Hengist's wife had found out about us and paid someone to scare me off. Then I got really paranoid and thought my mum had somehow worked out that I was at the church and had arranged it all to punish me.' She shrugged again. 'Or perhaps it was just some random burglar.'

Dad and I exchanged glances, shaking our heads, as stumped as she was.

'Or maybe that bitch Evangeline wanted to get rid of me. Her husband could have done it, couldn't he?'

Dad and Zillah left soon after that. I wrote a brief report for Julian, giving her the news that I'd found Zillah, concluding, *She is safe and well, and will contact you when she feels the time is right.* I had a feeling she was going to hassle me for Zillah's whereabouts, but I wasn't going to give way on that one: Zillah was an adult, and she had a right to privacy. My report also assured her that I was confident I'd soon unearth evidence that would prove Zillah's innocence. I attached an invoice for the hours I'd worked so far and pressed Send.

Though I was blagging it a bit, things *had* moved forward. Zillah had confirmed that Mindy had seen her and Hengist together. It was possible, wasn't it, that Mindy had picked up the rock and attacked him? Yes, she was slight, but she was fit and strong.

I flopped down on the sofa with a cup of tea, thinking over my conversation with Zillah and feeling that I'd missed something – but I didn't know what. I grabbed my notebook and scribbled down a rough outline of events.

- *Tuesday 14 September: Casting session for Jeeves Pulls it Off. Hengist arrives early and is heard talking to someone. Later that evening Hugh is pushed over and seriously injures his head when he falls on to a headstone. He's taken to hospital.*

- *Wednesday 15 September: I meet Zillah and reassure her she's unlikely to be suspected of having harmed Hugh. That night a man breaks into her flat, terrorises her and tells her to get out of her flat and not come back.*

- *Thursday 16 September: The next morning, Laurie arrives from Norwich, with keys to a beach hut and they start living there.*

- *Tuesday 21 September: First rehearsal of Jeeves Pulls it Off. Jem's van is seen near the churchyard, though he's supposed to be working in Sussex. Hengist stays behind after the rehearsal and meets Zillah in the churchyard. Janette, Dave, Iain, Betzy and Cedric leave at 10 pm. Bert sees a woman threatening Hengist with a rock. Mindy's plane to Budapest is cancelled. She goes to the churchyard, sees Hengist with a young woman, and they argue.*

- *At some later point, Hengist is struck on the head and dies.*

I stared at the list for a few minutes. I had a wealth of suspects, but no idea who actually killed Hengist.

I must have drifted off to sleep because the next thing I knew my phone was ringing. I snatched at it. Gwendolyn – sounding distant and ethereal

'I think I've seen the light. There's no need to worry about me. Not any more.'

And then she hung up.

I rang back but she didn't pick up – no surprise there. I considered trying to find her, but driving around the lanes of North Norfolk on a wild goose chase didn't appeal.

And she'd said that I didn't need to worry about her.

So I did something out of the ordinary for me. I lit a candle, sat quietly on a chair, and prayed for her to come back safe and well. You see, observing the fractured relationship between Zillah and Julian had made me appreciate some things about my mother. Yes, she was selfish. Yes, she'd been a neglectful parent at times, but she hadn't smothered me, or dominated me, or kept me imprisoned in a cult. In fact I could remember when I was about to go to university she'd kissed me and told me to spread my wings and fly. Yes, she'd been besotted with my half-brother, Tarquin, but she'd not mistreated me. She'd taught me how to make good coffee. She'd been the polar opposite of a conventional Stepford Wife. Her self-centred pursuit of her own interests, her own passions, was admirable, in a way.

In short, I was rather like her.

And though I didn't forgive her for how she'd treated Dad, I could forgive her for what she'd done to me.

38

In which Jem gets into a spot of bother

Jem Townley

It was Saturday lunch time and Jem was drowning his sorrows in The Bowling Green.

Friday had been the worst day of his life. First of all he'd had that awkward interview with the police and then Janette had dumped him.

How could she? They'd been together – what? – nearly two years, and hardly had a cross word.

Well, OK, they had had the odd niggle about Hengist. Christ, that slimy old lech was still causing trouble from beyond the grave.

After the police interview, they'd met for a drink in The Fleece. She hadn't hugged him or told him he had nothing to worry about. She'd been cool. Stand-offish.

Then she dropped her bombshell: told him she was moving to London in the next few weeks, and that he couldn't come with her. *It's for the best,* she'd said. *And in any case I'm going to stay with my aunt in Peckham and there's no room for you.* Then she'd gone into some crap about them having moved apart. Moved apart? Just a week ago they'd had the best sex ever, on the sofa in her lounge while her mum was out at work. Afterwards they'd lain there, arms round each other, naked, until he thought his heart would explode.

Because with Janette it wasn't just sex: it was love. He loved every little thing about her – her tidy ears, the way her hair went into a whorl on the top of her head, her fingernails, painted pearly pink, not like the scarlet talons of a former girlfriend which had gouged lines into his back. Plus she was smart and talented. Some of his favourite times were when they sat around watching anything featuring Sheridan Smith on catch-up, because Janette wanted to study her acting techniques.

After dumping him, she'd said she could only stay for one drink as she was taking her mum out for a meal.

And now his heart was breaking.

So he was gluing it back together with alcohol – pints of beer and Southern Comfort chasers. So what if it was the middle of the day? Fuck it. It was the weekend: he didn't have to go to work.

A man was coming in the door, silhouetted by the bright sun outside. Jem blinked, focussing as the lanky figure came into focus. Alfie Adams – someone else who'd been dumped on by Hengist. Granted, the man was a stuck-up git, but that was no reason for Hengist to treat him like a piece of shit, was it?

'Come over here, mate,' called Jem. 'Let me buy you a drink.'

After a moment's hesitation, Alfie came up to the bar, giving Jem his usual fake grin and perching on the stool beside him. 'Cheers.'

'What can I get you?'

Alfie rubbed his palms together. 'A pint of bitter would go down a treat.'

'I hear you got screwed over by Hengist. That's not fair, mate,' said Jem, as Alfie's pint was being pulled.

Alfie looked around nervously, but the pub was empty except for an elderly couple sat in a distant corner. 'I don't know if I'd put it like that, but he certainly led me up the garden path over the casting of Bertie Wooster.'

'He treated you like shit! I don't want to speak ill of the dead, but that's what he did.'

Alfie gave him another of those unconvincing smiles. 'Perhaps you're right. He could be a total bastard.'

'Let's drink to that.' They clinked glasses. 'Hey, let me buy you a short. Vodka, isn't it?'

'Well, if you ...'

Several drinks later Jem had decided that Alfie wasn't so bad after all. Yes, he was a prat, but he knew what Hengist was like. He understood. They'd spent a satisfying hour slagging Hengist off.

But as he looked into the dregs of his sixth pint, Jem felt tears rising into his eyes. He blinked them back, but Alfie was watching and touched him gently on the arm.

'You all right, mate?'

And Jem meant to say Yeah. Never better. Instead different words forced themselves out of his mouth. 'Janette and me – I think we're breaking up. And it's all my fault. Janette's an angel. And I'm a fucking idiot. She must have found out ...'

And his shoulders started to shake with sobs that couldn't be contained.

'She'll forgive you. She loves you, doesn't she?'

'I didn't mean to do it. I just got carried away. And now ...'

'Shhhh.' Alfie steered Jem to a quiet table, his hand gentle on Jem's arms. 'Whatever you've done, Janette'll come round. You'll see.'

Neither of them noticed the figure in a hoody drinking at the other end of the bar, listening to every word they said.

* *

Janette Tinker

Janette was sitting on their saggy sofa with her feet up, drinking a cup of tea when her phone rang. Jem. She glared at the screen; that was all she needed. But when it went to the answering service cries of pain and slurred words leapt out of the phone.

'Janette ... you've got to ... please, babe. Please ... I'm bleeding ... I've been such an idiot ... I didn't mean to ...'

Her heart contracted. She grabbed the phone. 'Where are you? What's happened?'

'St Nic ...' And then the line went dead.

The church. He was at the parish church. She leapt off the sofa and ran out of the door, fear running through her like an electric current. What had he done now? Had he tried to top himself? He'd been gutted when she told him he couldn't come to London with her. Said he couldn't live without her. She'd hardened her heart – hadn't given an inch.

Now look what had happened.

She ran down Wells High Street, turned into the churchyard of St Nicholas's and sprinted up the gravel path towards the main doors. But before she reached them she heard a moan coming from the longer grass around the side of the church. There! There, hunched up like a sack of potatoes close to the church wall, was a man.

Jem.

Dropping to her knees, out of breath, she saw that his

face was battered and bloody, the nose swollen and the lips split. A powerful smell of alcohol and vomit rose above the scent of crushed grass.

'Jem! I'm here,' she called, reaching for her phone to dial 999.

One eye, bloodshot bright scarlet, opened and fixed on her. 'I've done bad things. I need to tell you about them.'

39

In which Rags learns something that changes everything

Janette rang me while I was looking over my notes, wondering how to move the investigation forward.

'Someone's attacked Jem!'

'What? Is he seriously hurt?'

'Mainly his face. He's in A and E now, being stitched up. I'm outside, waiting to hear when I can go in and see him. He told me some things before the ambulance arrived.' I heard her swallow down a sob. 'He's not a bad person, you know. Just doesn't think before he acts.'

I waited.

'He says it was him who broke into that girl's flat – the one living at the church.'

'Zillah?'

'Yeah, that one. He says he never meant to harm her – just give her a fright.'

'But why?'

Janette sighed. 'He says she knew something about him, and he was afraid she'd talk.'

'But he didn't say what?'

'No.'

I was silent, mulling this over. At the back of my mind an idea started to form – a hunch that seemed far-fetched but which made sense of events.

'Does he know who attacked him today?'

'No. Some guy in a hoody dragged him into the churchyard and beat him up, but he never saw the man's face. Not properly. Look, I've got to go now. Can I ring you again later?'

As soon as she'd hung up my phone beeped: a message from Paddy McKee, my ex-Met contact who was an expert at ferreting out information, including that held by the police. He'd been away and non-contactable for the past week.

Back from the USA. Give me a bell.

Hallelujah. I rang him straight away. I gave him the low-down as quickly as I could, then gave him my instructions. 'I want to know anything and everything about certain people who were at St Botolph's that night. I'll text you the names and a few details. My client, Julian Lloyd, is paying, and I'm sure she'll run to a few hundred quid if it clears her daughter Zillah of any involvement in Hengist Bright's death.'

I felt a tingle in my fingertips when he said he'd get on to it ASAP. Things were moving forward at last.

After all this excitement I went out to the shops to pick up a few things, and walking home almost bumped into Evangeline, who had her head buried in a handkerchief and wasn't looking where she was going. It took me a little while to realise she was in floods of tears.

'Are you all right?' I asked.

She blew her nose loudly and glared at me through bleary eyes. 'Of course I'm not all right. I don't like being insulted. Not after everything I've done for that man.' She glowered at me as if I were responsible for whatever had happened. 'I even covered up for him so he wouldn't get into trouble. And what do I get in return? Insults. Abuse. I'm not having it any more.'

Paddy McKee rang me at eight the next morning.

'You're not going to believe this. Open up your email and see what I've sent you.'

I reached for my phone and what I saw made everything fall into place.

My first phone call was to Toots. We exchanged greetings and then I got to the point. 'In the photographs around the church, Hugh has long hair. When did he have it cut?'

'He still had his lovely locks a couple of weeks ago. Evangeline told me they had to cut his hair to treat his head wound, and then she tidied the rest of it up. A shame, really: I like a man with hair.'

'Thanks. That's all I needed to know.'

Then I rang Dad and ran through the broad outline of what I thought had happened to Hengist, and why.

He whistled. 'Are you sure, Rags? That seems pretty unlikely.'

'I know, but it's the only theory that makes sense.' I drummed my fingers on the table. 'I've got an idea. I'm going to get all the suspects together, then tell them what I think happened. And when I do that, I'm pretty certain we can unravel this whole thing.'

'How the heck are you going to do that?'

'Toots will help me. I'm pretty certain there'll be no trouble, but you'll be on hand to help out it if anything kicks off.' I thought for a moment. 'I'll ask Dave to keep an eye on things, too.'

'Can't you just tell the police?'

'There's no proof, Dad. I think the person responsible needs a little nudge to get them to admit what they've done.'

I could hear him thinking on the other end of the line. 'I suppose it might work.'

'If it doesn't, I'll turn everything over to the police. I promise.'

So I rang Toots again. 'I'd like you to set up a party – a gathering, if you like – of everyone who could be implicated in the murder of Hengist Bright. Do you think you could do that?'

'I don't see why not. My parties are legendary. People seldom turn down my invitations.'

'Even people like Mindy?'

Toots considered this. 'I could tell people it's a party to plan a celebration of Hengist's life and work, and to discuss the future of The Peasmarsh Players. Let me have a think about it. When do you want this party to happen?'

'As soon as possible. This evening, if Jem is out of hospital.'

'I went into the Deli and Janette told me he was discharged last night. He's sore but not seriously hurt.'

'Fantastic. I'll get on to Zillah. It's essential that she's there. And then I'll ring Hugh. If he knows she's going to turn up, he's bound to come. Can you manage the rest?'

'I reckon so. Let me have a go and I'll let you know if I need any help.

40

In which the Peasmarsh Players and others go to a party at Toots' house

And that, ladies and gentlemen, is how a gathering of people closely associated with Hengist Bright and The Peasmarsh Players came together that evening.

We met in Toots' house. Immaculate in a sleek black skirt, white silk blouse and turquoise loafers, she'd put on some quiet, moody jazz, and laid on freshly baked bread, cheese, ham and pickles. I'd sorted out wine, beer and soft drinks. We'd rehearsed what we were going to say, and I'd spoken to Jem earlier in the day, to make sure that he came ready and prepared to fess up to his part in the events at St Botolph's.

In my pocket I had the one piece of tangible evidence that explained a little of the riddle of what had happened at St Botolph's.

Hugh Blackthorn arrived first, in jeans and a blue linen jacket, looking tidier than when I'd last seen him.

Clean-shaven, his hair combed back off his face, he looked handsome and sober.

And nervous.

We'd had a conversation earlier on, and he'd confirmed certain facts, including his relationship with Hengist.

Evangeline came soon after him, her usual denim skirt paired with a stylish, embroidered jacket. As soon as she arrived, Hugh rushed over and reached for her hands. She pulled them away and stepped back.

'I'm so sorry,' he said. 'What I said was unforgiveable.'

She stared at him for a moment then allowed him to follow her to one of the sofas, where they conversed quietly.

Janette and Jem appeared next, clearly not the couple they'd been a couple of weeks before. His face had been patched up with tape and stitches but was swollen and badly bruised. Janette was immaculate in the black tights and denim shorts she'd been wearing when we first met at the casting session. Her hair, straightened, shimmered in golden sheets over a cream tee-shirt. She walked in with her back straight and her face unreadable.Mindy and Iain Bright arrived looking, pale, drawn. Toots welcomed them, murmuring condolences, and steered them to the second sofa.

Dave bounded in, dapper in linen shirt and faded jeans. He kissed my cheek and murmured, 'good to see you again,' in my ear. He smelt delicious.

Next at the door was Alfie, handsome as ever, but haggard. Following him was Betzy, draped in a funereal black skirt and blouse, though something smug about her expression suggested she fully expected to enjoy the proceedings.

Finally, Cedric arrived, gilded by a tan and a smile that suggested he was euphoric at being spared the need to embody the unflappable Jeeves. He apologised for being late, saying he'd only got home an hour ago, after flying in from Nice.

'So you've returned for my little gathering?' said Toots.

'Not quite. I have other things to sort out. But I'm delighted to be here: Hengist deserves a decent send-off.'

Dad was there, of course, and Napoleon, though not Susie, who was still visiting her sister in London. Napoleon made a beeline for Iain, sensing the boy needed comfort. I half expected Iain to shoo him away after the way he'd treated poor old Beckett, but before long he was stroking Napoleon, who settled down at his feet.

Zillah had arrived with Dad, before the others, and was upstairs in the spare bedroom, waiting to be summoned.

Toots served everyone with drinks; I stuck to spritzers. Then she clapped her hands and invited them to help themselves to food, after which we'd get on to the main business of the evening.

We'd decided to let them all eat and drink, to calm their nerves and lull them into a sense of security. Hugh ate little, and drank nothing but mineral water. Alfie drank like a fish and only picked at his plate of food, but then I'd already worked out that he was fond of amphetamines, and so had little appetite. The others tucked in – even Mindy and Iain, who seemed closer than they'd been before.

Once people had finished eating, Toots clapped her hands and thanked them for coming to plan a suitable memorial event for Hengist, concluding, 'But first Rags would like to say a few words about what happened on the night he died.'

A hush fell over the room. A shiver of nerves chased down my spine as I stood up, but I pulled back my shoulders and started in on the speech I'd been practising all day.

'Before we can properly celebrate Hengist's life, we have to know how he met his death. As some of you will know, the young woman called Zillah who was staying at the church until recently was seen at the churchyard that night, arguing with Hengist. But she wasn't the only person at St Botolph's after the rehearsal finished.'

Hugh jumped up from the sofa, dropping a fork in the process. 'Where is she? You told me she'd be here.'

'She'll be here later. I promise. Please sit down.'

Evangeline reached up and tugged at his shirt sleeve. 'Do as she says.'

'Mindy. You were supposed to catch a plane to Budapest that night, but the flight was cancelled. A Peasmarsh resident says she saw you in the churchyard that night. Were you there?'

She nodded wearily. 'Yes. I went there to surprise Hengist – to take him for a drink. But when I drew up, I saw him kissing a young woman with long fair hair – a woman I assumed was Janette, though now I'm not so sure. I yelled at them. The young woman ran away before I could see her face, and Hengist and I had a blazing row.' She looked round the room with tears in her eyes. 'He'd promised me he'd stopped all that – the tawdry love affairs and one-night-stands – but here he was, at it again. So I ripped into him. I told him our marriage was over. That I was going to divorce him.' She drew in a deep breath. 'He tried to placate me, saying I was imagining things, but I didn't believe him. I stormed off, drove home, and locked myself in the spare bedroom. I took a mild sedative so that I could get to sleep, then left first thing in the morning to catch an early plane. I didn't know whether he'd come home or not – we put our cars in separate garages – and I didn't care. Not then.'

'So when did you know that he was dead?'

'I got a phone call the next morning, while I was at the conference in Budapest.' She put her hands over her eyes for a few seconds then composed herself again. 'I can't forgive myself. If we'd left the church together that night he'd still be alive.'

Like a boy at school, Iain put his hand up. 'Can I say something?'

'Of course.'

Iain took a deep breath. 'When the rehearsal finished I went to the pub with Dave for a drink then drove home. I had nothing to do with his death. But we had quarrelled in the past few months. You see ...' He paused, taking a huge breath. '... I'm addicted to online gambling – have been since I was in my mid-teens, and because of it I got deeper and deeper in debt. In the months before Dad died I begged him for money, but he refused to cough up. He said I already had a generous allowance, and would just have to manage my money better or get a job. But I owed close on 20 grand. I was desperate.' He pulled a face which made him look younger, sweeter. 'You know what my dad was like. His drama productions meant everything to him, and he realised he could get me to perform in the play if he coughed up some dosh. So he offered me a grand if I took on the part of Bertie, because he was like that – desperate to win, to be the best. I agreed – of course I did – since it got the credit card companies off my back for a few weeks.' He paused to take a swig of white wine, gathering his strength to go on. 'And after Dad died I found a couple of his bank cards and used them to pay off more of my debts. How low is that?'

'Pretty low,' muttered Betzy, loud enough for us all to hear.

'And I'm sorry, mate,' continued Iain, looking at Alfie. 'If I hadn't taken Dad's bribe, you'd have got the part.'

Alfie gave a bony shrug. 'I don't know about that. I messed up *All My Sons.*'

'You're heading in the right direction,' said Dad to Iain. 'We all do stupid things – some of us for years on end. Just get on with sorting yourself out.'

Iain shot him a grateful look. 'Yesterday I came clean to my mother, and today I went to my first Gamblers Anonymous meeting. I'm starting to be honest about my addiction and make amends. Things are going to be different from now on.'

Mindy's hand reached for his, and squeezed it.

I thanked Iain then asked, 'Does anyone else want to tell us all what they were doing on the night Hengist died?'

A long pause followed before Jem stood up. 'It's time I spoke. I've been a complete arse. I've jeopardised my relationship with Janette and done things I'm ashamed of.'

All eyes turned towards him. 'I should have been in Sussex the night Hengist died. I was doing a big carpentry job down there with a pal of mine. I'd always thought there was something creepy about the way Hengist behaved to Janette, but a few weeks ago I started receiving anonymous texts hinting that there was something going on between them. First I ignored them, but these texts mentioned specific places and times when they'd met. I tried to talk to Janette, but she laughed and swore there was nothing going on – just extra coaching – that sort of thing. It got to the point where it was eating away at me.' He gave a long sigh. 'So I had the bright idea of driving back to Norfolk just to see if I could catch them at it, even though Janette had sworn that I'd got nothing to worry about.

'I arrived in Peasmarsh about 10 to 10 and parked up close to the church. I was so wound up I'd got a hammer out of my tool box and had it in my hand, though I swear I never intended to hurt Hengist – just to give him such a bloody fright he'd lay off Janette.

'But an old school friend of mine saw me and tapped on the van window. We talked for ages – he knew I was crazy about Janette – and eventually he made me see sense. We went off to a pub in Wells. I got totally pissed and wanted to go and see Janette, but he stopped me, thank goodness. I slept the night in the van then drove back to Sussex early the following morning. I swear that's the gospel truth. He can back me up.'

'And was anything going on?' said Mindy.

'No,' said Janette, loudly, a blush rising into her cheeks. 'Or not what you think. Hengist had persuaded me to go out with one of the judges of the play competition – flatter him, butter him up – so we'd have more chance of winning first prize. He said if I did that, he'd introduce me to an agent in London.' She pulled a face of disgust. 'I wish I'd never agreed to do it, but I was desperate.' She shook her head. 'Then I found out I didn't need him after all. I went to London under my own steam, and the agent has signed me up.'

I let Jem sink down into his chair. I knew there was more for him to say, but it could wait.

I looked round the room until my gaze settled on Cedric. 'Cedric? Do you have anything to tell us?'

Cedric gave a small smile – perhaps a smug smile. 'Nothing related to the night Hengist died. I drove home as soon as the rehearsal was over.' He allowed a dramatic pause to fill the room. 'But I do have something to tell you all: Sheila and I are getting divorced. I'm moving to the South of France. It's no secret that I didn't want to take part in *Jeeves Pulls it Off* but Hengist forced me into it. He'd found out from mutual friends that I'd started a new relationship ...' He let a pause hang in the air. ' ... with a man – Jean-Claude – whom I met in France while researching my latest book. Hengist threatened to tell Sheila if I didn't play ball. I was terrified of how she'd react so agreed to do one last play.'

'And? What's changed?'

'Jean-Claude persuaded me to be honest with Sheila.

And, yes, she's angry and hurt, but she's agreed to a divorce on reasonable terms.' Shaking his head, he continued, 'I've been a coward. She doesn't approve, but she's behaving in an honourable, decent way.'

Slow, contemptuous claps broke out: Betzy, with a sneer on her lips. 'Bravo. At last the only gay in the village makes it out of the closet.'

I turned to her. 'And what about you? Anything you want to tell us?'

'She and Hengist had some sort of past history,' piped up Mindy, eyeballing Betzy, daring her to deny it. 'He admitted as much to me once, after I asked him why on earth he kept giving her parts when her acting was wooden as a table leg.'

With a swish of her skirt Betzy stood up to hold the floor. 'Hengist Bright was a vain, poisonous man. He picked me up when I was seventeen years old, made me pregnant then forced me to have an abortion. Oh, this was long before you,' she snarled, pointing at Mindy. 'He was shacked up with some other woman with money back in those days. I was a student on a drama course at a community college in Essex. After he destroyed me it took me a decade to recover. But I did, and I went to work in the City and made a shed-load of money. Then I moved up here – I'd been keeping tabs on where he went – and, boy, was he surprised to see me. Didn't recognise me at first, because I'd had some work done on my face and lost a few stone. Then when he did accept I was who I said I was, we came to an arrangement: he'd give me parts in his productions, and I'd keep quiet about his past.'

'But that wasn't enough, was it?' I said. 'You wanted to ruin his life. You wanted revenge.'

Betzy gave me a sour grin. 'I never laid a finger on him.'

'Ah, but you had other means of making life difficult for him, didn't you? You sent those texts to Jem, didn't you?'

Betzy crossed her arms. 'I don't know what you're talking about. You can't prove a thing.'

I let that drop for now, and turned to Alfie. 'What about you? Were you there on the night Hengist died?'

His shoulders sagged. 'Yes. I got drunk and staggered up there to have it out with him – why he'd led me on then cast Iain as Bertie Wooster. I admit I was pretty out of it. I arrived around half ten to find the church hall closed up – I was so pissed I'd lost track of the time. I was going to sit in the churchyard for a bit, and sober up, but then I heard shouting and got scared. I didn't want to be involved in a fight – I just wanted to *talk* to him – to have my say, because it was all so bloody unfair.'

'And could you hear what they were arguing about?'

'Not really. Stuff like, *How could you?* and *That's disgusting. Sinful.* And then I heard what sounded like sobbing and howling. It scared the shit out of me, I can tell you. I ran back to Wells as fast as I could.'

I thanked him then turned to Jem. 'I think you've got something more to tell us, haven't you?'

With a groan, the bruised and battered Jem stood up again. 'Yes. You see, I wasn't just there on the night of the rehearsal. I was there the week before as well.' He rolled his eyes. 'Same thing. I was sure Hengist was hitting on Janette, and I wanted him to admit it.'

'And why were you so sure something was going on between them?'

'I'd had one of those messages on my work phone saying that Janette was a star-struck little slut who was carrying on with Hengist so she'd get a leading role.'

'So you went to St Botolph's and then what?'

'The auditions had finished and the place was locked

up. It was pitch black and to begin with I couldn't see a thing. But then I saw a man I thought was Hengist in the churchyard. He had his back to me and was walking towards the main gate. I saw red. I ran after him to give him a piece of my mind.'

'And?'

'And when I yelled at him, he ignored me. Didn't even turn round. So then I got really riled and went up behind him and shoved him in the back. He went down like a sack of potatoes, hitting his head on a gravestone on the way down. That bloody terrified me. I dithered for a bit, but then he got up and seemed to be all right, so I made a run for it. I drove back to Wells to meet Janette, and made up some story about being held up because I had to talk to a client about work.'

'Were you sure it was Hengist?'

'At the time, yes. But the next day in the Wells Co-op I saw Hengist and there was nothing wrong with his head. No bruise, no cut – nothing. I couldn't believe it. That was when it dawned on me that I'd injured an innocent stranger. Then I overheard Evangeline, who was in the queue for the tills, say that the vicar had been seriously hurt and realised it was *him* that I'd shoved. I felt sick with guilt, and should have gone to the police and confessed then and there, but I was scared I'd lose Janette.' He paused, hanging his head and taking some deep breaths. Janette was listening with an expressionless face.

'And then what happened?' I prompted.

'Evangeline was ranting on – everyone knows she's crazy about the vicar – and I heard her say that, Zillah, the girl who was staying in the church, probably knew something about it.'

'That got me thinking – got me in a panic, if I'm honest. I was shit scared that Zillah had seen what I'd done, and so

I went back to St Botolph's the next evening and ...'

'And you broke into my home and terrorised me, stole parish funds and planted an empty cash box in the apartment, so everyone would think I was a criminal,' came a voice from the doorway. Zillah stood there, pale and composed. 'I didn't see a thing, by the way. I'd gone to bed early.'

'I'm sorry.'

As he spoke, a roar arose from the other side of the room' How *could* you?' bellowed Hugh. 'She was an innocent child.'

'Sit *down*,' barked Toots.

'Yes. Please let me speak,' said Zillah. 'I'm not a child and I'm not innocent – not any more. But you wanted me to remain like that, didn't you? A child, dependent on you, needing guidance and protection. You couldn't stand it when I acted like a woman – an adult woman who had the right to love and be loved.'

'You don't understand!' shouted Hugh.

Zillah's shoulders slumped. 'I'd been having an affair with Hengist for the past few weeks after running into him one day while I was out walking. He was so charming. He listened to everything I said; he was interested in my life, my ideas. I'd never had anyone pay attention to me like that. He told me I was beautiful, special. To begin with we just talked. Then, one day he kissed me, and I ... I'd never felt that way before. Never. And, yes, I wanted it to go further.' She gave a little shrug. 'I suppose I was naive – I'd never had a relationship before – but I knew I loved him and I believed he loved me.'

She took a long breath. 'To begin with he didn't tell me he was married. Then he said he was, but that it was just a marriage of convenience. Then, a couple of weeks ago, on the night of the auditions, he rang me and said he was sorry, but we'd have to stop seeing each other. He sounded different: cold, distant. I couldn't believe it. And I wanted an explanation. I *deserved* an explanation.

'I wanted to talk to him that night, but he came with his wife, and I could see it was impossible. So I spent the evening in tears and had an early night.'

'And the next night you were attacked?'

'Yes. And afterwards I was so scared I threw some clothes into a case and ran off as soon as the man left. I rang Laurie, because I knew I could trust him, and he met me early the next day and sorted out the keys to a beach hut. But even after I was attacked, Hengist wouldn't see me. I sent him loads of texts, but he just kept putting me off.' She took another deep breath. 'So I told him I was pregnant and that he *had* to see me.'

'And he agreed?'

'Yes. We arranged to meet after the rehearsal.'

'And you took the pregnancy test result with you?'

'Yes.' She looked down at her clenched hands. 'I suppose I ... I wasn't thinking straight. I'd been stuck in that bloody beach hut for a week, feeling like death warmed up. In some part of my mind I hoped he'd leave his wife so we could be together. Then my mother wouldn't be able to get her claws into me again.' With a groan she dropped her head in her hands.

'But it didn't go as you hoped.'

She shook her head. 'He just kept saying that we couldn't be together. And when I begged him to tell me why, he said I wouldn't understand and started walking away. I was so furious I picked up a rock and ...' She sputtered to a halt.

'Did you hit him with it?'

'No! I swear by Jesus and all the saints that I did nothing to hurt him. He stopped, turned round and told me he was sorry he was such a lowlife. I dropped the rock, rushed over and kissed him.' Her head drooped. 'But it wasn't the same. The way he held me was more like a friend, or a brother. I was heartbroken. I started crying. He promised he'd sort things out properly once the production was out of the way.'

Dad and I both winced.

'He meant it!' said Zillah, eyes full of fire. 'I know he was selfish but he loved me in his own way. I know he did. He asked me where I was staying and I lied and said I was staying with a friend, because I couldn't face telling him I was living in a beach hut. Then his wife turned up, shouting at us. He promised to meet me the next day, in the woods behind the beach huts, and I ran off.'

'Did you hear any of their conversation?'

'No. Laurie had got hold of a bicycle. I cycled back to Wells as fast as I could.'

'And the next morning you found out that he was dead.'

Zillah looked up, eyes narrowed, and pointed at Mindy. 'Yes. And I bet *she* did it.' Mindy shook her head. 'I was angry with Hengist, but I would never have harmed him.'

The room fell silent.

'So who did?' asked Zillah, her voice on the brink of tears.

I looked at Hugh. 'Do you want to tell her, or shall I?'

Hugh took several long breaths then began. 'There's something you all need to know before I talk about the night Hengist died. I ... I ...' Tears came into his eyes as he stuttered to a halt.

'Go on,' said Dad.

'I'm Zillah's father.'

Zillah leapt up from the arm of the sofa, where she'd been perching. 'But you can't be! My mother told me that ...'

'When we were in our early twenties your mother

and I were both in a bit of a mess – drinking too much and hanging out in the park. Stuck in dead-end jobs, we spent most of our free time getting wasted. We weren't going out together – not properly – we were just part of the same group of friends that had hung out together since we were at school. But one night, after everyone else had gone home, things got out of hand and we made love. It was never meant to happen, and we never mentioned it again. We were ashamed: by then we were involved with an evangelical church that had strict rules on that sort of thing. I left Fakenham soon after that, not knowing she was pregnant. She didn't tell me about you until years later, when she made me swear on the bible that I'd never tell you or anyone else, but would stick to the story she'd told everyone. When you turned up at the church it was so difficult, loving you and being unable to be honest.' He fought back tears. 'I'd decided that I *had* to tell you the truth, whatever I'd promised Julie in the past, but before I could do that I had my accident and you disappeared.'

'So I'm your daughter? Really?'

'Really.'

She shook her head, as if trying to dislodge the thoughts and emotions buzzing around in there. A smile broke over her face, even as tears filled her eyes. 'I never believed I'd meet my father, and to know that it's you is the best news I've ever had.' Then her smile vanished. 'But why were you so angry when you found out I was seeing Hengist?'

Hugh took another deep breath. 'Because he's my brother. Our parents died in a car crash when we were kids and we spent our childhood years in different foster homes. Oh, it wasn't as tragic as it sounds, but we hardly knew each other. As teenagers we met up and started hanging out together. He was my big brother, and I loved him, but he was hard work: he always wanted to boss me around.

One day we were in the woods of the Holkham estate, mucking around with an air rifle, and I ... I shot him in the eye. Blinded him. I swear it was an accident. But he never forgave me.

'After that we were estranged for many years. He moved to London. I was consumed by guilt, and it took me years to straighten myself out. Then I found my vocation, went to theology college, and was eventually ordained.

'Meanwhile Hengist had changed his surname to Bright, because he thought it was more dynamic, and I changed my Christian name to Hugh, because I wanted to take the name of a Christian saint.'

'Go on: tell them your original name,' piped up Betzy, who was looking less bored as Hugh's extraordinary tale unfolded.

'We were christened Hengist and Horsa – legendary pagan Saxon warrior brothers. Anyway, one day I saw him and Zillah together at a pub in Castle Acre. From the way they were behaving I knew they were having an affair. The auditions were being held the next day, and I feared Hengist would use them as an opportunity to hitch up with Zillah, so I rang him immediately and told him that I was Zillah's father. First of all he wouldn't believe me. Then I think I convinced him and he promised he'd break it off. But ...'

'But what?'

'Then I had my accident and the next week is a blur. But I knew I'd talked to him, and needed to be certain he'd keep his word. So, after I was discharged from hospital, I went to the church on the night of the first rehearsal; I told Evangeline I needed to get some fresh air and walked up to Peasmarsh.' He took a deep gulp of breath and turned towards Zillah. 'And I saw you and Hengist together. But before I could reach you, Mindy turned up, and you disappeared.

'I waited in the shadows and after Mindy stormed off I tried to get him to swear that he'd finished with you. He said he'd already given his word and I was making a fuss about nothing. But there was something subdued about him; he wasn't his usual self. I was sure he wasn't telling me everything, so I grabbed hold of him. We argued. We fought. He blurted out that you were pregnant. And, yes, I howled and sobbed, because I was beside myself. He broke away and told me to stop being so childish. I was so furious I picked up a broken piece of gravestone and threw it at him.' His voice broke into a sob. 'I never expected it to hit him.'

'You were drunk,' came the dry voice of Evangeline. You'd been hitting the bottle for weeks, ever since Zillah turned up. And I tried to help you. I took away any booze I found in the vicarage, because I knew you were a good man at heart. I took you into my home after you were discharged from hospital, but you lied to me that night. Idiot that I am, I believed you'd been for a walk along the quay. I even told people you'd never left the house. May God forgive me.'

A long hush settled over the room.

Finally Zillah spoke. 'I can't condone the terrible things Hugh has done, but he took me in and gave me shelter. And I ... I've told lies, too.'

'Go on.'

'I suspected that Hengist was determined to finish with me, so I texted him saying I was pregnant so he'd have to agree to see me.' She paused and gave a long sigh. 'But I lied.' Then, looking at Hugh, 'So you don't have to worry about that.'

Hugh dropped his head in his hands. A moment later his shoulders started to shake with uncontrollable sobs.

After a moment, Evangeline took hold of his hand. 'You

didn't mean to harm him.'

'Yes, I did,' came the muffled reply.

'OK, but you never meant to kill him.'

A silence followed these revelations. Then Hugh cleared his throat and spoke again.

'I am, of course, going to ring the police and make a full confession, but before I do that I'd like to have the chance to talk to people, to start to make amends for the terrible things I've done, and how I've made them suffer.'

'When are you going to ring them?' said Dad, at his most stern.

'Before I leave this house,' said Hugh.

'Same here,' said Jem.

Dad gave them both a little nod and exchanged a glance with Dave, who called out, only half joking, 'I'll help you keep an eye on them. They're not going anywhere.'

41

In which Rags ties up a few loose ends

Hugh and Jem kept their word. Within half an hour they'd rung the police, and a car had arrived to take them both into custody. They'd be questioned in the morning.

The mood was subdued, but a palpable sense of relief ran round the room, helped along by generous helpings of wine for those who wanted it. Mindy retained a sense of dignity, holding tightly to the hand of her son, and talking now and then to people who came to offer condolences. Now the truth was out, it seemed The Peasmarsh Players were able to be more generous about Hengist.

Zillah sat beside Dad, who handed her a large handkerchief, and patted her hand every now and then. Napoleon abandoned his position beside Iain and came trotting over. After a small hesitation, she scooped him up onto her lap. I went over to ask if she was all right, and she said, in a shaky voice, that she was still in shock. 'No sooner do I find out the wonderful news that Hugh is my father than he confesses to killing his own brother. How can I

239

have a relationship with him now?'

'Remember that he's not a cold-blooded murderer. What he did was dreadful, but he never intended to kill Hengist.'

She blotted the tears that were running down her cheeks. 'I feel unbearably sad. And guilty. I've caused so much trouble. If I hadn't got involved with Hengist, none of this would have happened.'

'It wasn't your fault,' said Dad, firmly. 'Hengist took advantage of your inexperience, and your mother lied to you. If she'd told you the truth – that Hugh was your father – then you could have had a proper relationship with him, and he could have talked freely to you about Hengist. Don't go blaming yourself.'

'Thank you,' said Zillah, with a watery smile. Then, turning to me: 'I feel so foolish, deceiving people. When did you realise I wasn't pregnant?'

'Once you were staying with Dad, I started to wonder. My friends could hardly keep food down when they were first pregnant, but you were eating like a horse. So I looked closely at the test – I'd been so excited to find it that I hadn't looked at it properly before – and could see that you'd altered it.'

'I added the blue lines with a pen Laurie bought for me and covered them with some transparent nail varnish. I only ever intended to wave it under Hengist's nose to persuade him to come back to me. That was stupid, wasn't it?'

I didn't reply to this. I'd done plenty of stupid things, and felt I wasn't one to judge. 'Oh, I know what I meant to check with you,' I said instead. 'Does Hugh have a hearing disability? I think he was wearing a hearing aid when I visited him.'

She nodded. 'Yes. But he doesn't always wear it. He only needs it in certain large spaces.'

'Thought so. That explains why he didn't turn around

when Jem yelled at him, thinking he was Hengist.'

'And Hugh still had his ponytail then, so he looked very like Hengist from behind,' added Dad, fitting in another piece of the puzzle.

'What will you do now?' I asked Zillah.

'I'm going to start earning money and living an ordinary life.'

'And Laurie?'

'He's back in Norwich, saying he's going to try rehab again if he can get a place. I've arranged to meet him at the shelter next week. I might even start volunteering there again.'

'You know that if you do that, your mother might track you down?'

'If she does, I'll deal with it.'

After people had finally dispersed, I strolled with Dad and Napoleon to where his car was parked in Freeman Street, and waved them off. Then I moseyed back to Staithe Street, with a sense of satisfaction and the happy prospect of receiving a fat cheque from Julian in due course.

But as I approached the flat my pulse skipped a beat: there was a light on in the living room. Gwendolyn was back. I made my way quietly up the stairs. The flat door was ajar. I crept in, wary of what I might find.

'Darling!' a radiant Gwendolyn bounced over to me and gave me a hug. 'Look who's here.' She moved back to reveal a sheepish Nigel and my adorable brother Tarquin.

I burst into tears.

Tarquin fussed round me, handed over a cologne-scented handkerchief while Gwendolyn danced into the kitchen to open a bottle of the best Chablis 'to celebrate us all being together.'

241

'Thought I'd better come to your rescue,' said Tarquin, sinking down on to the sofa beside me and taking my hand. 'With the help of a techie wizard I tracked Nigel down in Las Vegas, and went to give him a stern talking-to.' He leant closer. 'He was missing her something rotten and longing to be given the push to come and get her.'

'And the pole-dancer?'

'That photograph was just a bit of fun. The truth is that Gwendolyn left the marital home after conceiving a massive crush on some phony guru who's set up shop a few miles from here. Nigel was so angry he thought he'd disappear for a while to teach her a lesson.'

Tarquin moved closer. 'And she was conned into handing over thousands of dollars,' he murmured in my ear.

Right on cue, Gwendolyn drifted over, a glass of chilled Chablis in hand. 'There you are.' She sank down on the other side of me. 'Isn't this delightful? The four of us together.'

'I've been worried to death about you,' I said. 'Why didn't you get in touch and tell me you were all right?'

'No reception, sweetheart.' Putting on a rueful expression, she batted her false eyelashes at me. 'I'm afraid I've been rather silly. I've been taken in by a charlatan.'

'But you never had an affair, did you?' chipped in Nigel.

'Of course not. I thought I was connected to him on a spiritual plain, but I was mistaken.'

I opened my mouth to say more, but was stopped by Tarquin squeezing my hand and announcing that he was going to be around for a week. 'I need to visit some London outlets, and you're coming to town with me. I've booked us rooms for two nights in a funky little boutique hotel near Kings Cross later this week.'

'Thank you,' I said, hugging him. Going to London with him was a more appealing prospect than going on my own, and while I was there I could meet up with my oldest friend, Carola, and do a bit of retail therapy on the funds Julian would provide.

We chatted for a bit longer, and then Gwendolyn announced that she and Nigel were leaving, 'to reconnect'.

Nigel grinned like the cat that's got the cream. 'I've booked us in at The Crown. Thank you for looking after your mother for the past couple of weeks.'

'It was nothing,' I said, feeling a twinge of guilt because I'd spent the whole of her visit wishing she was gone.

'And I'm off round the corner to a divine B and B run by a gay couple,' said Tarquin, yawning. 'We'll catch up tomorrow, when I've got over my jet lag, and make plans for our London trip.'

As I waved goodbye to them all at the front door, a message pinged into my phone. Dave. 'Fancy meeting up? I'm in the Fleece.'

'On my way.'

THE END

Acknowledgements

Huge thanks are due to Heather de Lyon, Zosia Wand and Barbara Stretch, who read drafts of the book and made perceptive comments. I'm also grateful to members of The Reading Room writers group who provided support and inspiration at our monthly meetings. Russell Holden at Pixel Tweaks designed the cover and the interior of the book, and gave excellent technical support. Special thanks must go to Heather de Lyon, who proof-read the book in its final draft.

Peasmarsh is a fictional location, but the lovely little coastal town of Wells-next-the-Sea is presented, I hope, with accuracy where actual names are used. However, all the characters and events are fictitious. In truth, the inhabitants of North Norfolk, including those who are involved in the many excellent amateur dramatic productions, are much kinder than some of those strutting their stuff in The Peasmarsh Players.

About the Author

Caroline Gilfillan grew up in Sussex, within earshot of the sea. She spent most of her young adult life in London, where she played music in various groups, including The Stepney Sisters, one of the first women-only bands. She was active in several inspirational writers' groups and after taking an MA in Creative Writing at Lancaster University, taught creative writing in universities and communities – work she absolutely loved. She spent a decade in North Norfolk before moving to Cumbria.

She's published five collections of poetry, including *Yes*, which won the East Anglian Poetry Book of the Year award. She received an Arts Council England grant to develop a novel set in the Second World War, which will soon be published. She's a winner of several national short story and poetry competitions. She's been involved in creative projects with the Paston Heritage Society, who explore and share the history of the Paston family in North Norfolk. A songwriter and musician, she performs in the South Lakeland area of Cumbria. To find out more, please visit www.carolinegilfillan.co.uk

Lightning Source UK Ltd.
Milton Keynes UK
UKHW011819091020
371320UK00001B/89

9 781999 609764